"Smart as you are, Mr. Gallagher, you don't know everything."

"Are you always this much trouble, Officer Murdock?"

"Pretty much."

They weren't touching, but they were both breathing hard as the furtive exchange of tempers and opinions mutated into a different kind of heat. Their breaths mingled and their chests nearly brushed against each other with every inhale. Her head filled with the spicy scent of shaving cream or soap on his skin. Her body warmed with the proximity of his body lined up with hers. She wasn't even aware of the holster poking into her backside anymore. Quinn's gaze fixated on her lips and Miranda couldn't look away from those laser blue eyes.

But she did. She had to. It was time she remembered why she was here—and the little girl she'd been hired to protect.

JULIE MILLER

NANNY 911

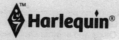

TORONTO NEW YORK LONDON
AMSTERDAM PARIS SYDNEY HAMBURG
STOCKHOLM ATHENS TOKYO MILAN MADRID
PRAGUE WARSAW BUDAPEST AUCKLAND

Thank you to MaryAnn McQuillan.

You opened up your big heart and your busy schedule
to take pity on my sore fingers and computer frustration.
Thanks for retyping the manuscript for me!

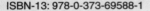

Recycling programs
for this product may
not exist in your area.

ISBN-13: 978-0-373-69588-1

NANNY 911

Copyright © 2011 by Julie Miller

ABOUT THE AUTHOR

Julie Miller attributes her passion for writing romance to all those fairy tales she read growing up, and to shyness. Encouragement from her family to write down all those feelings she couldn't express became a love for the written word. She gets continued support from her fellow members of the Prairieland Romance Writers, where she serves as the resident "grammar goddess." This award-winning author and teacher has published several paranormal romances. Inspired by the likes of Agatha Christie and Encyclopedia Brown, Ms. Miller believes the only thing better than a good mystery is a good romance.

Born and raised in Missouri, she now lives in Nebraska with her husband, son and smiling guard dog, Maxie. Write to Julie at P.O. Box 5162, Grand Island, NE 68802-5162.

Books by Julie Miller

HARLEQUIN INTRIGUE

*THE PRECINCT
**THE PRECINCT: VICE SQUAD
‡THE PRECINCT: BROTHERHOOD OF THE BADGE
‡‡THE PRECINCT: SWAT

CAST OF CHARACTERS

Quinn Gallagher—CEO and genius behind Gallagher Security Systems. A self-made billionaire whose inventions have revolutionized police and security work around the world. A man whose success got his wife killed, and is now endangering the one love left in his life, his daughter.

Miranda "Randy" Murdock—Sharpshooter with KCPD's premier SWAT Team 1. Tough and highly-trained. This tomboy has the skills and determination to prove herself in a man's world, but she's out of her depth when it comes to masquerading as a nanny for an adorable little girl...and falling for her charge's widowed father.

Fiona Gallagher—Three years old. Curious and feminine and crazy about her daddy.

Louis Nolan—Quinn's right-hand man at GSS. He keeps the investors happy.

David Damiani—He runs security at GSS headquarters.

Elise Brown—Quinn's executive assistant is loyal to the company. Or is it her boss she's so attached to?

Ozzie Chang—A lab geek at GSS. Quinn sees a lot of himself in the young man.

Nikolai Titov—GSS's largest foreign investor.

Vasily Gordeeva—Quinn's father-in-law has been in prison for a long time.

John Murdock—Randy's big brother is a Marine stationed overseas. But he's had a second career bailing his kid sister out of trouble.

Prologue

"Start the countdown."

The armed driver in the modified camo uniform floored the accelerator, forcing his five passengers to hold on for their lives as they bounced over the ruts and sand and scrub brush of the arid terrain. "I recommend waiting until we get to a safe distance."

The one person not wearing mock military garb clung to the Hummer's passenger seat. "And I recommend you follow my orders to the letter. That's why I'm paying you, isn't it?"

"Part of my job is to protect you. There could be fall-out here."

"I didn't come all this way to miss the show. I want to be here at the beginning, just as I'm looking forward to being there at the end—when I see his face and can revel in his failure." The anticipation of seeing that arrogant face downcast in broken sorrow, his eyes filled with tears, his clipped voice perhaps begging for mercy, was enough to make one light-headed. Or maybe it was this bone-jarring ride across the Kalahari that was affecting rational thought. The boss gripped the door handle and dashboard and turned to the driver. "Push the button."

Surrendering to the inevitable winner in this battle of wills, the driver pulled the tiny remote-control switch box from his shirt pocket and activated the countdown. He set the device in his lap, but refused to stop the vehicle. Supposedly, that was the sign of a good leader— putting the safety and well-being of his team first. Too bad not every man in this world believed that.

"Another mile between us and the facility won't make any difference on this terrain." The driver slowed his speed a fraction and handed over a pair of military-grade binoculars, ironically designed by Quinn Gallagher, owner of the facility that was growing smaller and smaller beyond the swirl of dust in the vehicle's side-view mirror. "Here. Take these. You'll be able to watch the sweat beading on their foreheads when they realize they've got no place to run or hide."

"You're certain there are only the guards at the gate?"

"You know, for someone who has planned some seriously scary stuff out to the last detail, you're pretty squeamish about collateral damage."

"I'm not afraid to kill someone if I have to." The raging injustice and bone-deep pain swirling through the passenger's heart made it far easier than even the mercenary driver could imagine to inflict pain without feeling remorse. "But I don't want a high casualty rate. Too many outsiders would get involved then and he'll lock down tighter than one of his vaults. Because I've mapped my strategy down to the last detail, I need to maintain control of the situation. To do that, each task must be completed the way I've directed."

It was a lesson that had been learned the hard way—that there were steps, deadlines, terrible costs for not getting everything just right. It was a lesson that could never be forgotten.

"You're the boss."

"Don't you forget that." The enemy had. That was why he had to pay. "If he thinks I'm going to stand by and let him ruin my life, he's mistaken. I intend to hurt him as badly as he's hurt me. And I intend to strike where it will hurt him the most."

"It's almost time."

"Stop the car."

With the advantage of higher ground on the mesa where they'd stopped, the view of the facility was unobstructed. The boss adjusted the binoculars to watch.

"Five, four, three, two—"

The boss held up a hand, demanding silence, wanting to savor this first triumph.

It started as a rumble, a sound so deep they felt the tremors through the ground, vibrating up through their feet and legs seconds before hearing the first pop. Then there was a flash of light, followed by that distinctive whoosh as the initial ignition in the plant's disposal chamber sucked all the oxygen from the surrounding rooms. There was a split second of silence, the anticipation leaving them all holding their breaths.

And then...*boom. Boom. Boom!* One by one the explosions fired off, each one larger than the last, tearing through the shiny new facility, spewing flames and steel and glass into the air. Thick black smoke coiled upward, forming dense black clouds against the desert's crystal blue sky. In a matter of seconds, there was nothing left of Gallagher Security Systems's newest production facility except mangled webs of steel and burning rubble.

The team of mercenaries watching alongside had done their job well. The boss lowered the binoculars and watched it burn, feeling the heat even at this distance.

The satisfaction was intense.

Payback had begun.

Chapter One

7 Days until Midnight, New Year's Eve

"Someone is trying to destroy me."

Quinn Gallagher touched the temple of his dark-framed glasses, an ingrained habit left over from his youth, when he'd been a four-eyed brainiac from a rural Missouri trailer park who'd learned how to defend himself and his mother from the respective bullies who'd preyed on them. He was no longer poor, no longer had his beloved mother—and up until the murder of his wife, Valeska, nearly three years earlier, he'd believed that he no longer feared anything.

Now three employees that he'd never met, but for whom he certainly felt responsible, were dead in a foreign country. And the office building that he'd closed for the holidays, with paid vacations off for all but the skeleton crew of security guards receiving overtime pay, was being searched from basement to rooftop by a team of black-uniformed cops, armed like the special-ops security details his company outfitted for wealthy individuals and companies across the country. The captain of KCPD's SWAT Team 1, Michael Cutler, often served as a consultant to GSS when they were developing new weapons, protective gear and security technology.

He was also one of the few men in this world Quinn Gallagher trusted without question. He strode into the penthouse office suite with a disturbing yet unsurprising announcement. "Thus far, we've found no sign of forced entry into the building or your office. I've got my team checking the top floor here now. Of course, this place is locked up tighter than Fort Knox. Whoever got in had to have the same kind of talents you possess." It was a wry compliment. An enemy with Quinn's technical skills would be a formidable opponent, indeed. The SWAT captain turned toward the small, unwrapped Christmas present Quinn had left on his desk. "Don't let me or my men interrupt your meeting."

"Come and go as you need, Michael. Thanks." Quinn adjusted the knot of his silk tie and paced the length of his office. The men and woman in suits on the matching sofas waited expectantly for some sign that he was ready for their problem-solving input. But none of them dared offer any personal condolence or sympathetic look. He paid them exceedingly well to be the best at the jobs they'd been hired to do, not to be his friends. That was a bonus he rarely bestowed on the people around him. Caring had cost him dearly—when he'd lost his mother, and three years ago when he'd lost his wife.

He didn't need the distraction of emotional ties to interfere with the efficiency of this Christmas Eve meeting. And his people knew that. Keeping an eye on Michael Cutler and the furtive movements of the rest of his five-man team through the chrome-and-glass partition separating his office from the rest of the floor, Quinn turned his attention back to the executives who'd been able to report on such short notice.

Louis Nolan, his vice president of operations and Quinn's eyes on every aspect of Gallagher Security Systems, was speaking. "I've already been on the phone with Nikolai Titov, our primary investor there. He wants answers."

"He'll know them as soon as I have them," Quinn promised.

"The Kalahari plant hadn't even begun production yet," Louis continued. "We were still in the hiring process with the locals. I know we were building there to save money, but now we're posting a loss on GSS's bottom line and facing speculation from the press. Titov's already putting the pressure on to let him reopen and expand the St. Feodor plant in Lukinburg. The last thing we need right now are nervous stockholders. I think we should entertain his offer before this unfortunate incident turns into a catastrophe."

As Quinn suspected, his security chief, David Damiani, wasted no time pushing to his feet and confronting the older businessman. "Unfortunate? I lost three good men in that explosion. Try making that phone call to their families when Christmas is tomorrow."

"I'm not denigrating the loss of life." Louis was a cagey old salt who had no problem defending himself. "I'm pointing out that this could be an environmental or political attack on GSS's expansion into South Africa. I know our base of operation here in Kansas City is thousands of miles away, but this could snowball into a real tragedy if we don't spin some control over the situation in the next few days, if not the next few hours."

David raked his hands through his hair, the movement exposing the Beretta he wore holstered beneath his left arm. "It's already snowballing, Lou. How do you explain someone breaking into GSS headquarters when we've got the best damn techno-security on the planet? I can't. As far as I can see, we're already under attack."

"Gentlemen," Elise Brown intervened. Quinn knew his executive assistant could be counted on to keep everyone focused and moving forward. "None of us are thrilled to be taken away from our families and vacations at this time of year, and certainly none of us are pleased to hear about sabotage and the murder of GSS employees, but you're missing the point. Quinn said someone was trying to destroy *him,* not GSS." She turned her soft brown eyes up to him. "Isn't that right?"

"Yes." That was the painful distinction he'd made. Going after his business empire was one thing. But the gift-wrapped package he'd received on his desk this morning…

His gaze drifted over to the shiny red paper and white tissue decorated with candy canes, of all things—his daughter's favorite holiday treat. Quinn seethed inside, momentarily experiencing that same helpless fury that had plagued him growing up, before he'd learned to use his brain as a weapon to outsmart the kids who'd picked on him and the men who'd thought his mother didn't have anyone to protect her.

He forced his gaze away from where Michael Cutler was processing the unwanted gift with his gloved fingers. He looked out the floor-to-ceiling windows, over the stone-gray parking lot, highways and wintry fields around the modern building he'd erected near the Kansas City International Airport north of the city center. The isolation he felt made the glass windows, marble tiles and Oriental rugs seem especially cold and sterile today. He'd mistakenly thought he'd left the users and abusers of the world far behind him in that small-town trailer park. Instead, after the destruction of his South African plant two days ago, Quinn realized that he'd simply graduated to a more ruthless, more covert class of users who wanted to hurt what was his.

He wasn't so naive to think he hadn't made a few enemies over the years. At forty, he'd already earned and lost one fortune. But now that he'd established himself and his company as a world leader in high-tech security support and management, he was sitting on an even bigger fortune and had enough influence across several different industries that only a fool—or one very sick, very cruel bastard—would dare to defy him.

Judging by the message he'd received this morning, he was opting for the latter.

"What? Now? I'll be right there." Elise had pulled her cell phone from the coat she'd tossed over the sofa beside her. The distress in her tone was enough to divert Quinn's attention. Her eyes darted to him, then just as quickly looked away. More trouble? "Excuse me."

"Ma'am." An oversize SWAT cop, carrying one of the electronics-scanning devices Quinn himself had invented, stepped aside to let Elise exit the door into the privacy of her office. The big man, who answered to the name Trip, settled in behind the desk to run a check on the phone and computer for any hint that someone had downloaded entry codes to the building and offices.

One by one, the rest of Michael's team filtered in. Quinn traded a nod of recognition with the SWAT team's second in command, Rafe Delgado, whom he had met when he'd offered him the use of a secure safe house for his wife, the witness who'd finally identified the man who'd murdered Quinn's wife. Rafe introduced himself to David Damiani and took the security chief aside to discuss possible incursion scenarios into the building.

A short, muscular cop with curly black hair came through the doorway next and reported in. "Murdock and I have got nothing, Captain. This place is locked down tighter than a tomb. This room and the roof are all that we have left to search. You want us to head on up?"

"Have Murdock check the cameras in here for any signs of tampering. You go on up, Taylor. Stay warm."

"Yes, sir."

Officer Taylor turned his Benelli shotgun and disappeared from the doorway, only to be replaced a moment later by an unexpected colleague. Quinn's eyes narrowed as he found himself studying the last member of Michael Cutler's elite team. He didn't know if the long ponytail, as straight and shiny as a palomino's tail, or the Remington sniper's rifle strapped over her right shoulder surprised him more.

"Captain?" she spoke.

"Front and back, Murdock. If we can't find an unauthorized access point to this room, then we damn well better find where the perp covered his tracks." Michael Cutler pointed to the two cameras at either end of the room, and after her moss-colored eyes took note of every person here, including him, Officer Murdock's long legs carried her to the security camera mounted over the bar/kitchenette at the back of the office.

"Yes, sir."

Quinn watched her climb on top of the counter in her ungainly boots and shimmy around a counter to stand eye to eye with the camera. He couldn't be sure if it was her monkeylike athleticism and disregard for the obstacles in her path or the hint of firm hips and buns in her snug black pants that fascinated him.

Annoyed with his scientist's penchant for observing and explaining conundrums like the well-armed woman, Quinn cursed under his breath and summoned the focused business mogul inside him instead. The momentary diversion of the lady SWAT cop was a distraction he could ill afford today. There was only one female in his life who mattered, and she was the reason Quinn had called Michael Cutler and his team, as well as the leaders of his own staff, into GSS today.

Quinn buttoned his jacket and strode over to stand beside Captain Cutler at his desk. "Did you read it?"

The words Michael read were already branded into

Quinn's memory. But the others in the room—his staff, Michael's team—needed to hear this.

"Do I have your attention now? Your daughter will pay the price if you don't make things right by midnight on New Year's Eve. Instructions will be texted to you." Michael carefully slipped the letter into a plastic evidence bag for examination in the KCPD crime lab. "And you received the text?"

"Not yet. I wanted to have a plan in place before he contacted me again."

"Any idea who your enemies are?"

"Any idea who they aren't?" Louis Nolan pushed himself up off the couch to join the conversation. "I'm sorry, Quinn, but we'll be here all day if we start compiling a list of people you've ticked off—employees you've fired—"

"Only with just cause."

"—business rivals, greedy cutthroats after a chunk of your money, maybe even a brokenhearted lover or two?"

Quinn shook his head. "There's been no one since Val."

Louis patted Quinn on the back and raised one eyebrow in a skeptical, paternal look. "Not for lack of trying. On the part of the ladies, I mean. A widowed billionaire makes for a fine catch."

"This reeks of inside information—someone with building schematics, someone with knowledge of my schedule, someone with access codes to this building as well as the plant in South Africa. The fact that I have enemies doesn't bother me as much as not knowing who this particular one is." And he hated to admit that the possible list of suspects Louis referred to was as long as it was.

Quinn had fended off takeover bids, negotiated with foreign governments and endured scathing reviews of his products in the press. He wasn't a warmonger, nor did the upgrades to weapons and protective technology he owned dozens of patents for turn the police patrolling the streets of Kansas City and other towns around the world into a military state. Everything he invented, every product his company produced, from home security systems to bulletproof flak vests, was designed to keep people safe. He protected people. The same way he'd learned to protect himself. And his mother. The way he'd protected his wife, Valeska, from the violence of her past—only to have her die at the hands of an obsessed serial killer in the backyard of the home they'd once shared together. A home he'd since razed to the ground and replaced with a fortress more secure than the government buildings his company sometimes equipped.

Nothing, no one, would ever harm his remaining family again.

That was why he wasn't above calling in favors from KCPD and summoning his most trusted associates to the office on Christmas Eve. "This building is supposedly more secure than the Cattleman's Bank. So how did someone get into my office and put this here without anyone seeing the perp, or capturing the intrusion on one of my cameras?"

Trip Jones, the big guy with the electronics scanner,

rose and circled the desk, with David Damiani, the GSS security chief, right behind him. "I can't see anything that's been tampered with on this end, Captain. There's no indication on the key cards that anyone other than Mr. Gallagher has entered this office in the last twenty-four hours. If there's no record of a break-in to leave the present, then the perp found another way in and covered his tracks."

Officer Murdock climbed down from the file cabinet where she'd been inspecting the other camera. "There's no indication that either of these cameras has been compromised."

Trip nodded. "Then the tampering must have occurred at the monitor end of things. Digital recordings can be altered as easily as a videotape."

David Damiani's team had already determined as much. "That means you're accusing one of my people of delivering that threat."

"No one's accusing anyone of anything." Michael Cutler coolly defused the growing tension between the two security forces. "Yet. Let's just get all the intel we can first. Arm ourselves as best we can so we know what we're up against."

"Sounds like a smart strategy," Quinn agreed. He nodded to David. "Check it out."

"Quinn." David Damiani was right to protest. GSS wasn't a billion-dollar corporation because it gave away its secrets to outsiders. "There's classified equipment in my offices."

Michael Cutler refused to back down. "You're obstructing a police investigation?"

"He's obstructing nothing," Quinn countermanded. When the threat involved his three-year-old daughter, nothing else mattered. "David, go with him. Give Trip full access. Maybe between the two of you, you can spot something your guards missed."

"Yes, sir."

While Quinn impatiently waited for the info that could give him the answers he needed, his gaze strayed once again to the woman with the flak vest, Glock strapped to her right thigh and sniper's rifle secured over her shoulder. She was over at the windows now, trailing her fingers along the chrome trim.

Louis Nolan had followed her to the windows, his bushy silver brows knitted together with the same perplexed interest plaguing Quinn. "They'd have to rappel from the roof and cut a hole in the glass to get through that way."

She nodded, studying the seam of the window from top to bottom. "It could be done. I could do it."

"Unless you had a fear of heights," Louis teased.

"Fortunately, I don't."

"I'll bet you don't fear much, do you, darlin'?"

The blonde officer's cheeks flushed a delicate shade of pink. Carrying numerous deadly weapons and crawling across his furniture didn't fluster her, but a *darlin'* from a good ol' Texas charmer did?

Quinn stopped the conversation. This wasn't the time for Louis's flirting. Or his own scientific observations. "I think we'd see the evidence if someone had come through the window. Beyond the fact that it's tempered, shatterproof glass and the condensation outside from the freezing temperatures would make any kind of traction for your climber almost impossible, there's no way to replace that specific kind of window overnight."

She turned her wide green eyes from Louis, seeming to understand his facts better than his COO's flirting. "Is there another exit to the roof besides the stairwell next to the elevators? Anything with direct access to your office?"

"No."

She tipped her chin up toward the ceiling "What kind of duct work do you have running up there?"

Officer Murdock was definitely an odd sort of woman, certainly nothing like the polished beauty of his executive assistant, Elise, or any of the other poised and tailored belles he escorted to society events. "Standard issue, I suppose. Although the access panels do have sensors to monitor whenever one opens or closes."

Michael Cutler seemed to think she was onto something. He looked up at the air-return grate over Quinn's desk. "Murdock. Call Taylor down and scout it out. Looks like there's more than one way to get into your office, Quinn. The right perp could even lower the package through that grate without ever setting foot in here."

The bothersome blonde paused by the desk on her way out the door. "Couldn't the break-in be something more simple? Like, someone you know—someone who wouldn't raise any suspicions if they were caught on camera walking into your office?"

Quinn bristled at the accusation. "The people who

work at GSS are family to me. I surround myself with people I trust without question."

"Well, that's a problem, then, isn't it?" She flipped her ponytail behind her back, looking up at him with an earnest warning. "You may be trusting the wrong guy."

"Randy, go."

Her captain's brusque command finally moved her out of the room. "Sorry. Climbing into the rafters now, sir."

Apparently, Louis's interest in waiting for answers on the break-in—or for the promised text message— waned once she'd left the room. "I'll be in my office if you need me," he excused himself, "and *do* call as soon as you find out anything."

"Randy?" Quinn asked after they'd both gone and he was alone in the office with Michael.

"Miranda Murdock." The police captain shook his head, as if Quinn's wasn't the first curious reaction the SWAT sharpshooter had garnered from the people she met. "Believe me, what she lacks in tact, she makes up for in sheer determination. There's not a task I've given her yet that she hasn't accomplished."

"Other than successful public relations."

"She's raw talent. Maybe a little too eager to get the job done at times. She matched the highest score for sharpshooting on the KCPD training range."

"You have faith in her."

"She wouldn't be on my team if I didn't."

"Quinn?" The familiar knock at his door told Quinn

that his assistant, Elise, had an important message for him.

"What is it?"

Elise tucked her dark hair behind one ear, hesitating as she walked into the room. Quinn braced for whatever unpleasant bit of news she had to share. "The current nanny has gotten wind of the threat against Fiona and wants to quit."

He adjusted his glasses at his temple, snapping before he could contain a flash of temper. "I'm having a Mary Poppins moment here. How many nannies do I have to go through to get one who'll stay?"

"She's afraid, Quinn."

"There's a guard with Fiona at all times," he argued.

"Yes, but not with the nanny," Elise patiently pointed out. "Quinn, she has every right to be concerned for her safety. The guard's first duty would be to Fiona, not her."

Where was the loyalty to his family? The sense of responsibility? The devotion to his daughter? She was the fourth woman he'd hired this year—after firing the one he'd caught drinking at the house, and the one who thought spanking his three-year-old was an option, and filing charges against the one who'd tried to sell pictures of his daughter to a local tabloid. "Where is she now? I'll double her pay if she stays."

"Um…"

"Daddy!" Quinn understood Elise's hesitation when the tiny dark-haired beauty who looked so like her late mother ran into his office.

"Hey, baby." Quinn knelt down to catch Fiona as she

launched herself into his arms. He scooped her up and kissed her cool, wind-whipped cheek as her long, thin fingers wound around his neck. "How's my little princess today?"

"'Kay." Even though she couldn't read yet, he turned her away from the hateful note on his desk and bounced her on his hip. Fiona batted away the gloves that were clipped to the sleeves of her coat and held up her well-loved, oft-mended hand-sewn doll. Fiona's bottom lip pouted out as she pointed to the bandage taped to the doll's knee. "Petwa has a boo-boo."

Quinn pulled up the cloth leg and kissed it, suspecting he'd find a similar first-aid job under the knee of Fiona's corduroy pants. Although the initial flush of her cheeks had concerned him, he was relieved to see that Maria, the nanny du jour, had at least taken the time to dress his daughter properly for the winter weather and brush her curling dark locks back into a neat ponytail before abandoning her.

"There. She'll be all fine now." Stealing another kiss from Fiona's sweet, round cheek, Quinn set her down and pulled off her hat and coat. He nodded toward the specially stocked toy box he kept behind the counter of the kitchenette at the far end of his office suite. "Okay, honey. You run and play for a few minutes while I talk to Elise."

"'Kay, Daddy."

He waited until the box was open and the search had begun for a favorite toy before he turned his attention to his assistant. He didn't have to ask for an explanation. "The nanny didn't call," Elise told him. "She dropped

Fiona off with me downstairs and left. I couldn't convince her to stay."

Quinn unbuttoned his jacket, unhooked the collar of his starched white shirt and loosened his tie, feeling too trapped from unseen forces and ill-timed inconveniences to maintain his civilized facade. He paced down to see with his own eyes that Fiona was happy and secure, playing doctor on her doll with a plastic stethoscope and thermometer.

He came back, scratching his fingers through his own dark hair. He needed to think. He needed answers. Now. "Can you watch her, Elise? I have work to do. I don't want to leave until I resolve this threat."

Elise's mouth opened and closed twice before her apologetic smile gave him her answer. "For a few hours, maybe. But my parents are in town, Quinn. I'm supposed to be baking pies with my mother, and taking them to the candlelight service at church this evening. Besides, I can't keep her safe. And if that threat is real…"

He had no doubt that it was. Three dead men in the Kalahari proved that. "You could come to the house. You know what kind of security I have there. There's a panic room and armed guards."

"And my parents?" He'd always admired Elise for her ability to gently stand up to him. "It's Christmas Eve, Quinn."

He was already nodding, accepting her answer, knowing it had been too much to ask. "Of course. I understand. I was just hoping I wouldn't have to upset Fiona's routine any more than it already has been."

The vibrating pulse against his chest ended all conversation, blanked out all thought except for one more visual confirmation that Fiona was safe. Then he let the protective anger he felt purge any distraction from his system as he pulled his phone from inside the pocket of his suit jacket.

"Quinn?" Michael prompted, equally on guard.

He nodded, reading the message he'd been promised. "It's the text."

"What does it say?" Elise asked.

Quinn read the skewed nursery rhyme, filling in the abbreviations as he said the words out loud. *"Mary, Mary, Quite Contrary, how does your money grow? With silver bells and 2.5 million shells into 0009357:348821173309. Midnight tonight. Or there'll be another present for your daughter."*

"What the hell?" was Michael's reaction.

"It's a riddle," Elise needlessly pointed out.

"I get it," Quinn assured them. "Mary was my mother. I have a memorial trust in her name. Whoever this coward is wants me to transfer two and a half million dollars into this account by midnight. Or…" He glanced over at Fiona's laugh. He couldn't imagine a world where someone had silenced that glorious sound. "I'll transfer the money."

"I don't recommend that." Michael took the phone from him, calling his tech guru Trip on the radio to get him up here to trace what Quinn was certain would be an untraceable number.

"What choice do I have, Michael? How can I fight the enemy when I don't know who he is? And until we do find out where the threat is coming from, there's no way to stop him from coming at me again." He turned to his assistant. "Elise, contact my bank. Don't let them close before I get there."

"Yes, sir." She hurried to her office to do his bidding.

Michael copied down the message. "What if you hadn't understood the rhyme?"

"I don't think this bastard is stupid. And he knows I'm not."

Michael pointed toward the letter wrapped in the evidence bag. "This message says to make something right before New Year's Eve. That's a week away. It can't be this simple, and he's gone to too much trouble to have it all be over this soon."

"Agreed." Quinn propped his hands on his hips. "As long as I can keep Fiona out of this, I want to string this guy along until I can get my hands around his neck."

Any further conversation stopped as the grate over Quinn's desk swung open and Miranda Murdock lowered herself down through the opening to plop her combat-style boots on top of his desk. She'd stripped off her Kevlar and rifle and was brushing dust from her black uniform and snaggled hair. And she didn't seem to see anything odd about making such an entrance.

"I think I found the way in, sir," she reported to Michael, jumping down beside him. "Barring the whole 'just walking through the front door' scenario. Of course, the intruder would still have to alter the camera recording—and turn the sensors off for the few seconds it would take to get in and out." She paused in her report, her sharp eyes turning to the side and widening enough that Quinn turned to see what had caught her attention.

Fiona. Standing in the middle of his office, her doll dangling to the floor beside her, looking up at the tall blonde woman as if a dusty angel had just descended from heaven.

Miranda's lips twitched before settling into a smile. "Hey."

The tiny frown that creased Fiona's forehead gave her an expression that was more concerned than afraid, or even curious. "You falled."

The SWAT officer looked up at the open grate, still swinging slightly from the ceiling where Fiona was looking. "Um, no. I crawled. And climbed. And… jumped." She plucked a clump of cobweb from her hair, glancing toward Quinn and her commanding officer with a questioning plea before pointing a finger at his daughter. "But, you shouldn't try that. It's too high. I'm, you know, taller. And a grown-up."

But the explanation had taken too long and Fiona had moved on to her real concern. Quinn's hands curled into fists at his sides as Fiona walked right up to Miranda and held up her doll. "Petwa falled."

"Oh. Um, well…" She snapped her fingers. "That's exactly why you shouldn't crawl through ceilings."

Fiona stared.

Quinn gradually relaxed his protective stance. Not everyone got small children, nor knew how to communicate with them—and he suspected Miranda Murdock was on that list. But he could see she was doing all she could to allay Fiona's worries.

"Not that your dolly—Petra, is it?—would do that. She needs to stay close to you. On the ground." Seemingly as flummoxed by his daughter's fascination as she'd been with Louis's idle flirtation, she looked to her captain for help. "Sir?"

Michael nodded a dismissal. "Prove to me that you can get back out through that heating duct, and I'll have Trip check the sensors there to see if they've been triggered by anyone else in the last twenty-four hours."

That, apparently, she could do. Needing no more encouragement, the twenty-something female officer climbed up on the desk and pulled herself back up into the ventilation duct in a skilled combination of pull-up champ and gymnast.

"She's...different, isn't she?" Quinn observed.

"Like I said, Murdock is gung ho. She'll get the job done."

"Michael." Quinn usually found his instincts about people to be unerringly accurate. "I have another favor to ask of you. Just how much faith do you have in Miranda Murdock?"

Michael's blue eyes narrowed. Perhaps he'd just had a similar brainstorm. "You've supplied my team with nothing but the best equipment since we first started working together. Your vest design saved my life from a bullet once. I figure I owe you."

"Then I have a proposition for you." Quinn scooped Fiona into his arms, drawing her attention away from the dusty blonde angel and the grate that had closed over their heads. "*We* do."

Chapter Two

Miranda stilled her breathing, calmed the twitchy urge to blink and squeezed the trigger of her Glock 9 mil, landing five shots, center mass, through the paper target's chest. Then just for good measure, and because the accuracy score of her shooting range trials was one thing she could control, she angled the gun and put a hole through the paper target's head.

"You shouldn't be alone at Christmas," Dr. Kate Kilpatrick advised. The police psychologist was always full of advice during their sessions. "If your brother is still over in Afghanistan—"

"He is."

"—then maybe you could volunteer at one of the city mission shelters, visit a shut-in in your neighborhood or invite a friend over for lunch."

And just which of her friends would be available on Christmas Day? Certainly none of the men on her team. They all had families—wives, children, in-laws. They'd be real gung ho about giving up holiday family time to keep the "odd man out" on their team from being alone *on Christmas Day. Lonely was one thing. Pity was another.*

Miranda pulled off her earphones and pushed the button to bring the hanging target up to the booth for a closer inspection. Instead of heeding Dr. K's recommendation to find some company after her mandated counseling session that afternoon, Miranda had come to KCPD's indoor firing range in the basement of the Fourth Precinct building to blow off steam.

All that touchy-feely stuff Dr. Kilpatrick wanted her to talk about got stuck in her head and left her feeling raw and distracted when they were done. Randy Murdock was a woman in a man's world. Her brother, John, a KCFD firefighter who'd reupped with the Marines after the love of his life had married someone else, had raised her to understand that when the job was tough—like being a part of KCPD's SWAT Team 1—that what she was feeling didn't matter. Four other cops, and any hostages or innocent bystanders, were counting on her to get the job done. Period.

No warm fuzzies allowed.

Nodding with satisfaction that her kill rate had been 100 percent, Miranda sent the target back and cleared her weapon.

"What are you thinking?" Dr. Kilpatrick asked after a long, uncomfortable silence.

"That I'm not the only person with such a nonexistent home life that I'm available for an appointment the afternoon before Christmas."

"Ouch." Observant though it was, Miranda regretted the smart-aleck remark as soon as she'd said it. But

the therapist let it slide right off her back with a poised smile. "There you go deflecting the focus off yourself again. Deftly done, too. I could write an article about your classic avoidance tendencies. Always striving to please someone else instead of working toward your own goals. Using work or physical activities to avoid thinking about your feelings or dealing with the lone-liness."

Sharp lady. Miranda hated that the police shrink might be onto something there. "So why are you here at four o'clock on Christmas Eve, Doc?"

"To see you, of course."

"Sorry about that." Miranda pushed herself up out of the cushy seat. "We'd better wrap things up then, hmm?"

"Miranda, sit." Dr. Kilpatrick wore a maternal-looking frown now. And though she'd never known her own mother, or maybe because of that, it made Miranda feel so unsure of how she should respond that she sank back into her chair. "You're just as important as any of the other officers, detectives and support staff here in Kansas City."

"Yeah, that's why I'm the low man on the totem pole on my team."

The maternal vibe became a supportive pep talk. "That's nonsense. You're a highly qualified sharp-shooter. You passed all the same rigorous physical and mental exams as the other members of your team. Other than chain of command, you know it takes all five of you working together equally and complementing each other's strengths to make SWAT Team 1 the success it is."

Miranda released the magazine from the Glock's handle and pulled out the remaining blanks. Then she reloaded the clip with 9 mm bullets from the ammo box on the shelf in front of her and ensured her gun was in proper working order before returning it to the holster strapped to her right thigh.

She was in the locker room showering when more of the conversation she'd had with the psychologist started replaying in her head.

Dr. Kilpatrick had the patience of a saint. She could ask a question and wait. But the ongoing silence in the psychologist's office finally got to Miranda, and she blurted out one of the few things that scared her. "Holden Kincaid is coming back."

"Kincaid? I know several Kincaids on the force. Which one is he?"

"He's the guy I replaced on SWAT Team 1 when he went on paternity leave. He and the guys are all pretty close." The random confession had sounded like polite conversation to fill the silence at first. But once one insecurity was breached, others came out. *"I mean, even if I prove I'm as good at this job as he is, possibly even better, what good does that do me? If Captain Cutler and the guys resent that I'm there instead of him, that messes up our efficiency. I'd feel like a real usurper for being there. But if I transfer off the team, or get cut because Kincaid is a better man..."*

She turned off the hot water and hugged her arms around her naked body as the water ran down the drain and the locker room's cool air raised goose bumps across her skin. If Dr. Kilpatrick wasn't so good at her job, then Miranda might not still be shaking from the embarrassing accuracy of the psychologist's next question.

"Do these self-esteem issues go back to that incident this summer when the Rich Girl Killer attacked you?"

"He wasn't after me. He wanted Sergeant Delgado's girlfriend—his wife now—because she could ID him."

"I read Delgado's report myself. He said you slowed down the RGK long enough for him to get there to save his wife from being murdered."

Backhanded praise was no better than a reprimand. *"My job wasn't to slow him down. It was my job to stop him. I failed. He got the drop on me, bashed my head in and I failed."*

"There's a reason it's called a team. It takes all of you, working together, to complete your mission. You're there to complement each other's strengths, and, on certain days, compensate for a weakness. Every man on that team knows that. Every man has been where you are. No one blames you for having an off day."

That indulgent, don't-be-so-hard-on-yourself tone only made the self-doubts whispering inside Miranda's head shout out loud. *"You know it's different when you're a woman, Doc. 'Good' isn't good enough. If I can't perform when my team needs me to, then why the hell should Captain Cutler keep me around?"*

The psychologist jotted something on her notepad, then leaned forward in her chair. *"SWAT Team 1 is your family, aren't they? That's why you're being so hard on yourself, why you're so afraid of making a mis-take. You don't want to lose your family again."*

Stupid, intuitive psychologist! That was why the session with Dr. Kilpatrick had upset her so much today. She'd gotten Miranda to reveal a truth she hadn't even admitted to herself yet.

With her parents both gone and her older brother stationed in Afghanistan, Miranda had no one in Kansas City. No one, period. All she had was this job. Being a cop—a highly select SWAT cop—was her identity. It gave her goals, satisfaction, a sense of community and worth. If she screwed it up, then she'd really be up a creek. Of course, the holidays only exacerbated that reeling sense of loneliness she normally kept at bay.

And she'd actually revealed all that to the doctor?

"Ow!" The pinch of sanity on her scalp told her that (a), she was tugging too hard with the hairbrush, and (b), she needed to get a grip. If she wanted to make the claim that she was a strong woman who deserved to have the job she did, then she needed to quit wallowing in these weak, feminine emotions that felt so foreign to her, and get her head on straight.

Decision made. Time to act. Emotions off.

"Now get out of here, Murdock," she advised her reflection in the mirror.

After pulling her long, straight hair back into a ponytail, Miranda dressed in her civvies and bundled up in her stocking cap and coat to face the wintry air blowing outside. Night had fallen by the time she hurried down the steps toward the crosswalk that would lead her to the parking garage across the street.

Heading south for half a block, she jammed her hands into the pockets of her navy wool peacoat and hunched her shoulders against the wind hitting her back. When she reached the crosswalk and waited for the light to change, she pulled her cell phone from her pocket to check the time. Great. By this hour on Christmas Eve, none of the usual restaurants where she liked to pick up a quick dinner would be open. She tried to picture her freezer and wondered what microwave choices she had on hand that she could zap for dinner, or if she'd be eating a bowl of cereal again. Why couldn't she remember these things before she got hungry and the stores had closed?

The light changed. She jumped over the slushy gray snow that had accumulated against the curb, and hurried across the street. That was another thing she missed with John being over in Afghanistan. Besides the bear hugs and patient advice, the man could cook. She'd never really had to learn because he had the gourmet talents and interest in the family. Miranda could easily recall the ham, mashed potatoes, baby asparagus, fruit salad and thick chocolate cake John had fixed for Christmas dinner last year. Her mouth watered at the memory of silky, semisweet frosting and light, moist layers of pure fudge heaven.

Her bowl of cereal was sounding pretty sad right about now.

She entered the parking garage and jogged up the ramp to the second level, where she'd parked her red pickup that morning, long before they'd gotten the call to the Gallagher Security Systems building. As the morning's events passed through her mind, her thoughts took a left turn and landed on the image of GSS's boss, Quinn Gallagher, running the show in his poshly furnished, high-tech penthouse office.

The tailored suit and way he spoke, straightforward and concise, as though he was used to people jumping at his word, were clear indicators of his wealth and power. But the short dark hair with that one shaggy lock falling out of place onto his forehead, and those Clark Kent–ish black glasses said science geek. Surprisingly, there'd been muscles under that suit coat. She'd seen them flex and push at the seams of his jacket when he picked up his little girl. Quinn Gallagher was an odd combination of a man—a nearsighted nerd with guns and pecs hidden beneath his suit and tie.

Miranda grinned at the inside joke of her own making. Did Mr. Gallagher even know that he resembled a famous comic book character?

"What's so funny?"

Stifling the startled gasp that tried to escape, Miranda halted at the big man climbing out of a truck parked in the row across from hers. The black KCPD sweats marked him as a friend, but recognition made it difficult to keep her feet from dashing to her own vehicle. Talk about lousy timing.

"Hey." Lame greeting, but sufficient. Holden Kincaid needed no introduction. She shrugged off the sappy grin that had caught his attention. "Private joke. About a comic book."

"It's Murdock, right?" He pointed to the proportionately sized silvery malamute circling the bed of his truck. "Yukon, stay." Amazingly, the dog sat on his haunches as his master crossed the driving lane to extend his hand. "Holden Kincaid."

"I know who you are, Officer Kincaid." There was nothing but polite friendliness in his demeanor, so running away from the man whose return to duty was giving her such fits about her job would only broadcast the insecurity she needed to hide. With the workout sweats, stocking cap and scarf tucked around his neck, she could guess he wasn't here to take her job this evening. "Going for a run?"

He nodded, thumbing over his shoulder at the dog. "Ol' Yukon there loves the snow, so any chance we can do a winter run, we go for it."

Keep it natural and conversational. "Even on Christmas Eve?"

His laugh clouded the chilly air. "Liza said I needed to get out of the house for a couple of hours. I take it there's some Santa Claus stuff in the works with her and my son. So I took the dog out for a run, then came here to lift weights in the fitness center. I figure they need about another thirty minutes before it's safe for me to go home."

Liza must be the wife. Friendly man. Obedient dog. Family at home. Miranda's isolation burned like a giant hole opening up in her belly.

"Well, I won't keep you from Santa Claus."

"Wait a sec. Murdock?"

"Yeah?"

When she turned to face him again, his smile had

turned into a wry frown. "I'm glad we ran into each other."

Right. So she was naive to think she was the only one who felt there was a competition between them. He was trying to make the best of an awkward situation. She should be mature enough—confident enough—to do the same. She pulled her ponytail from the collar of her coat and tossed it down the middle of her back, busying her hands for a moment to calm her nerves. "Yeah, well, it was bound to happen. I mean, you're back from leave, and I'm...always here, apparently."

With something like a sigh of relief, Kincaid's smile returned. "Captain Cutler said you were a bit of a workaholic."

Guilty as charged. "I like the rush of the job, I guess. I feel useful. I'm in my element."

"I know what you mean. I love being home with my wife and the baby, but I'm anxious to get back to it."

Great. So she and Holden Kincaid were kindred spirits with similar talents. They might have been friends under other circumstances—if he wasn't gunning for her job; if she hadn't taken his in the first place.

She glanced around the nearly deserted garage and tried to make an exit again. "Well, um...Merry Christmas."

"Murdock." This time Miranda kept walking. "Look, I just wanted to say this isn't how I wanted it to happen."

She opened her truck door, but stopped at the odd remark. "Wanted what to happen?"

Her cell phone rang in her pocket, but she was more

concerned about deciphering the apology stamped on Holden's expression.

He nodded toward her coat pocket. "You'd better take that."

"What are you talking about?"

"Your phone. It may be Captain Cutler." He started backing away. "If so, it's important."

"How do you know...?" An ingrained sense of duty pushed aside the ominous vibe that this *chance* meeting with Holden Kincaid had nothing to do with co- incidence. Too many phone calls in her life meant a summons to an emergency, and seeing Michael Cut- ler's name on the screen of her phone indicated this was a call she couldn't ignore. She climbed into her truck, closing the door as she hit the answer button. "Yes, sir?"

With a "Merry Christmas, Murdock," Kincaid turned and jogged down the ramp and disappeared around the garage's front gate into the night.

"I didn't catch you in the middle of dinner, did I?" her commanding officer asked. The friendly greeting told her this wasn't an emergency.

So Miranda took the time to start her truck and get the heater running before answering. "This is a good time to talk. What's up?"

"We've had a situation develop over the course of the day at Gallagher Security Systems that requires your... unique expertise."

"A situation?"

With a muffled curse, the captain cut the chitchat and got straight to the details. "I talked to Sergeant

Wheeler about your schedule this week. She said you volunteered to take some extra patrol shifts over the holidays so that some other officers could spend more time with their families."

He was calling her on Christmas Eve over this? "I've already cleared it with the desk sergeant. It won't count as overtime. I'm just trading my vacation days for another time."

"It's an admirable gesture, but I took the liberty of clearing your schedule for the next week. I've already talked to Holden Kincaid, and he'll take the shifts you were going to cover so no one else has to change their plans. The team is on On Call status this week—if something comes up, he'll fill in for you."

A bolt of icy electricity rippled down Miranda's spine and her gaze shot to the black pickup in her rearview mirror. *This isn't how I wanted it to happen.* Kincaid's words made sense now. He'd already known he was replacing her—not on SWAT 1, not yet—but that was what the preemptive apology was about. Cutler had already made the arrangements to get her out of the picture.

The gray dog sat in the back of the truck, watching her. He'd probably known his master was here to take her place, too.

She clenched her fist around the steering wheel as those insecurities that had plagued her since the Rich Girl Killer screwup shivered through her. She was losing the job she loved, losing her *family,* as Dr. Kilpatrick had put it. Only a girly-girl would sit here and cry about it. Still, the inevitable feelings of loss, betrayal and failure burned beneath her eyelids.

"Randy?" Captain Cutler was speaking in her ear. "You still there?"

Tearing her gaze away from the dog and turning off those self-sabotaging emotions, she managed to keep an even tone as she answered. "I'm here, sir. Why don't you want me to work over the holiday?"

"I don't want you to work patrol," he clarified. "Since you're not traveling out of town, I'm recruiting you for a dedicated assignment this week. And you *will* be receiving overtime pay for the extra hours."

Pay was the last thing on her mind at the moment. "What's the team going to do at Gallagher Security?"

"Not the team, Randy. You."

"Well, can't Holden take the assignment instead of covering for me?"

"No. He can't." The normal clip of authority in his tone softened to something slightly more paternal. "I'd consider it a personal favor if you do this for me. Can you meet me tomorrow? After you're done with whatever plans you have for Christmas morning?"

Miranda's sigh filled up the cab of the truck. She was available after a bowl of cereal tonight if he wanted. Besides, doing a personal favor for the captain couldn't hurt her chances of staying on SWAT Team 1 now that Holden Kincaid was back in the picture. "I'll be there."

She jotted down the address he gave her and promised to meet him at noon.

What kind of assignment was she good enough for, but Holden wasn't? Or was it a case of what assignment was Kincaid too good for, but she was adequate enough to fit the bill?

Stop it, Murdock. Miranda willfully shut down that negative voice in her head and disconnected the call. Dr. Kilpatrick might have her pegged better than she'd given the psychologist credit for. Her confidence really had been rattled by recent events.

Miranda shifted the truck into Reverse and pulled out of her parking space. When she braked to shift into Drive, she took a moment to scan her surroundings. There might be skeleton crews working over the holidays at KCPD, but none of them had parked up here. There wasn't a soul to be seen. It was just her and the unblinking malamute who watched her drive past. And the dog didn't count.

She was alone on Christmas Eve. No one was here to see her drive away; no one was at her apartment to welcome her home. Her boss had some sort of mysterious assignment that would separate her from the rest of the team for a week.

One might think she'd have gotten used to going solo through life by now.

But she hadn't.

It stank.

Chapter Three

6 Days until Midnight, New Year's Eve

What was she doing out here in the middle of this ritzy new subdivision on the northern edge of Kansas City on Christmas Day?

The homes were spread out on tracts of land, each one big enough to be a city park, with tall, old trees lining the road, and well-established landscaping, despite the newness of the construction of the multistory, sprawling mansions she could see from the road. Her whole apartment could probably fit into the garage of one of these places. Heck, it could probably fit into one closet. She was a long way from her home in downtown Kansas City in more ways than one.

Miranda checked the address in her hand one more time before turning her truck into the short driveway that marked the entry to Quinn Gallagher's estate. Unlike the other estates she'd passed, there was no part of the house visible from the street until she pulled right up to the front entrance. Taking note of the cameras set on either side of the front gates, she peeked through the wrought-iron bars. There was a secondary set of gates recessed behind the decorative entrance. They looked solid, like steel doors that could come together to completely close off the front entrance. And from this vantage point she could see that the masking effect from the street had more to do with the height of the brick walls surrounding the property rather than the mansion being smaller than any of the others in the area.

Almost austere in its offset, multitiered design, the white house was set well back from the road, with a frozen creek that acted almost like a moat circling around it. The only thing breaking up the lines and angles of the numerous windows and long porches were the ropes of colored lights and greenery decorating it for the holidays. With a foot of snow on the ground, the undisturbed lawn on either side of the long, curving driveway created a sea of white. Approaching the house without being seen would be nearly impossible. It was probably an architect's dream home, or, more likely, the brain child of a man obsessed with security for himself and his family. Snow drifted three feet deep at the base of the tall brick walls on either side of her, and nestled on every leaf of the thick ivy covering the barricade, completing the illusion of an impenetrable ice palace.

"The Fortress of Solitude," she mused out loud, wondering if Quinn Gallagher had read the same comic books she had growing up. Either he was clueless about the whole steely-man-hidden-beneath-the-nerdy-exterior persona he projected, or he possessed a tongue-in-cheek sense of humor and was actually playing up the similarities to the incognito superhero.

Then again, maybe she was the only one in a five-mile radius who noticed that the gazillionaire inventor turned businessman resembled an icon from her youth.

Ignoring the random thought, Miranda rolled down her window to press the call button on the intercom system outside the gate. As she leaned out, her eyes went to the black BMW parked in front of a giant evergreen wreath at another set of estate gates farther down the road. It wasn't unexpected to see an expensive car with a driver in this part of the city. It wasn't unusual to even see the tinted windows that masked whoever was riding in the backseat.

But it was Christmas Day and she'd been the only traffic moving through the neighborhood since she'd turned off of I-435 near the airport. And if that was someone visiting a family member, why park in the street? Why not pull up to the gate as she had?

Maybe they were lost and stopping to read a map or check a GPS. It was a plausible explanation.

"Yes?" The unidentified voice over the intercom demanded her attention.

Apparently, friendly greetings weren't standard procedure here. Miranda followed suit. "Officer Murdock from KCPD. I'm here to meet with Captain Cutler and Mr. Gallagher."

"You're expected."

She heard a metallic snap, a motor firing up and then the distinctive sound of gears grinding against each other. Retreating from the cold, she rolled up her window and watched the heavy gates slowly slide apart.

She might have shifted into Drive and readied her truck to drive on through if some little sixth sense hadn't pricked the hairs at the nape of her neck. Never one to ignore such a cosmic warning, Miranda subtly angled her head to check her mirrors and windows.

A woman so used to being alone had fine-tuned the instinct to notice when she wasn't. Her gaze went back to the black BMW.

They weren't lost.

They were watching her.

Or maybe watching the Gallagher estate?

As soon as she turned in her seat to look head-on at the lurking car, the backseat window rolled up and closed, giving her a glimpse of silver hair and pale eyes staring in her direction. The window hadn't been cracked open before. Someone was definitely checking her out.

And there was no excusing the passenger's curiosity as an effort to decide whether or not to approach her. The car with its unseen occupant suddenly sped up and drove past.

Instinctively, Miranda kept her truck in Park and blocked the entrance to the Gallagher estate. It wouldn't be the first time an opportunistic thief or terrorist or whatever threat waited inside that car seized the opportunity to enter a locked-down area by tagging along when someone else opened the door. But the BMW never slowed. In a matter of seconds, it had turned the next corner and disappeared over a hill leading back to the highway.

But not before she'd pulled a notepad and pen from the center console of her truck and copied down the license plate number.

"You coming?" the voice from the intercom asked. "Drive forward so we can lock the gates."

"Yes, sir."

Tucking the plate number into her coat pocket, Miranda shifted into gear and pulled forward. She steered around the first curve of the driveway and headed toward the bridge decorated with multicolored lights and garland that spanned the frozen creek. A mysterious car with a curious passenger might be nothing important.

But a SWAT officer left nothing to chance.

"BABYSITTING?"

Quinn finished the calculation he was figuring and typed the variables into the laptop on the desk between him and the leggy blonde sitting beside his good friend Michael Cutler. He adjusted his glasses as he glanced from Michael to Miranda Murdock. Had he not explained himself clearly?

He zeroed in on the curious mix of shock and resentment darkening the mossy-green irises of Officer Murdock's eyes. She looked intelligent enough to understand the situation. This wasn't going to work if the woman had an attitude, either. Surely Michael wouldn't recommend her or have her on his team if she was a problem. "There's a distinction, Miss Murdock."

"It's *Officer* Murdock."

"My mistake, *Officer.*" He wished he had options besides Blondie here right about now. "I'm hiring you to protect my daughter until the threats against us have been resolved."

"Wait a minute." Her booted feet hit the carpet and she leaned forward in her chair. "I work for KCPD. You can't just hire me away."

For a split second, Quinn's multitasking mind wandered away from both his calculations and the irritating need to clarify himself. For that split second, his brain filled with observations about Miranda Murdock's black uniform and how not even the mannish turtleneck or starched collar could detract from the natural blush staining those sculpted cheekbones. And her long hair, pulled back with an eye toward practicality rather than style, was more than just blond. He detected variations of honey and wheat and sunshine in the strands framing her face. Very pretty coloring all round.

A pesky voice cleared its throat inside his head. Why was he noticing a woman all of a sudden? Why was he noticing this one? He had a wife. So the key word was *had,* since Valeska had been killed three years ago, shortly after Fiona's birth. His New Year's resolution in January had been to finally put away the wedding ring he hadn't been able to take off. He hadn't made any resolutions yet for the upcoming year about starting a new relationship, or even considering candidates who'd be eligible for one. This argumentative tomboy certainly wouldn't be suitable.

Move on.

Just like that, the moment passed. Thoughts of his wife's murder and the veiled threats against his daughter and company negated any fanciful observations about a woman's subtle beauty and focused him firmly on the business at hand. He nodded toward the SWAT emblem embroidered above her chest pocket and returned to his calculations. "You can't wear that outfit around Fiona."

"I earned the right to wear this uniform."

"And you should be commended for that. But my donation to the KCPD Widows & Orphans Fund gives me the right to decide how you dress around my daughter. I don't want her frightened or put off by the military-looking attire." Quinn completed his calculations and plugged them into the new parameters he'd been texted this morning. "She likes jewel-tone colors. Do you have anything like that you could wear? Jeans or slacks are acceptable over the holidays."

"Jewel-tone…?" Her unadorned cheeks were blushing again. Temper, he suspected, not embarrassment. "Do you want me to paint my gun fuchsia pink?"

Quinn swung his gaze over to his friend for help. "Michael?"

This conversation had already taken more of his time than it should have. He had a deadline he needed to meet here. Hours after he'd transferred the money from his mother's trust fund into the unmarked Swiss bank account, he'd received the next threat. Rework the blueprints on a remote-access lock he'd designed several years ago. It was an old system that was no longer in use with any of GSS's customers, so it didn't pose a security breach to GSS or any of its production facilities. But Quinn didn't ask why the unidentified caller wanted him to waste his time on this today. It was enough that the caller had threatened to deliver another present for Fiona by the end of the day if Quinn didn't comply.

Complete the task or it will be Fiona's last Christmas.

Protests or not, refitting the old design by 5:00 p.m. made gaining Miranda Murdock's cooperation of the utmost importance.

Michael Cutler had seen the text. He understood the threat. Maybe he could get Officer Attitude there to understand. "This *is* a police matter, Randy. Quinn and Fiona are Kansas City citizens whose lives and livelihood have been threatened. With GSS's connections to KCPD, as well as to global security, the commissioner has asked us to form a protection detail to stay with the family 24/7 until we get this straightened out."

"Through New Year's Eve," Quinn added, prepping the design for an online trial. "24/7 until January 1. And then..." His stomach somersaulted as he thought of his beautiful little princess playing with her presents in the adjoining family room. He prayed he'd be able to right whatever perceived wrong this bastard was accusing him of by New Year's Eve. He wished his unseen enemy had come straight for him instead of involving Fiona in this sick countdown game. But then the creep must have known that there was only one way to get Quinn to do exactly what he wanted—threaten the love of his life.

He felt the moss-green eyes on him as he watched the dark-haired little girl putting stickers over all of her green velvet dress, and on most of the furniture in the room.

"A protection detail I get." He detected a softness in Officer Murdock's voice that hadn't been there a moment ago. But when he turned to meet her curious gaze, she looked away to speak directly to Michael. "I'm happy to watch the premises or assist his security staff. Maybe we could start by putting a live guard on the front gate. With the way the security cameras are positioned, there was no way for the man inside at the monitors to spot the BMW parked in the next block and scoping out the place."

"What?" Quinn's alert level ratcheted up another notch. "You saw a car watching the estate?"

"I couldn't see much of who or how many were inside—other than an older man in the backseat. They drove away as soon as I showed an interest in them." She turned to Michael again. "I've got the plate number if you think I should run it."

Michael took the paper she pulled from her pocket. "I'll handle that. Quinn, do you want me to…?"

Quinn had already dialed David Damiani's number at the estate's security office. "David. I need you to run an ownership and identification check for me on a…" He pointed to Officer Murdock.

"Black BMW."

"…on a black BMW." He signaled Michael for the license number. "Missouri plates C3K-49F. It's not one of your guys, is it?"

"In a Beemer? No, sir."

"Then get one of your men out to the front gate. My KCPD guests spotted the car watching the estate earlier."

"Will do, boss." Damiani was brusque, but thorough. "I'll put Hansen on it and get out there to check it myself."

Quinn hung up. He pulled off his glasses for a moment and rubbed at the headache forming between his eyes. Then he slipped them back on and looked directly at the woman who might just be exactly what he needed, after all. "Now do you see why I need you to be a part of my household this week? I can't afford to miss anything that could impact my daughter's safety."

"You want me to go undercover as the nanny for your little girl."

"I want you to *be* her nanny. That means staying with her 24/7, seeing to her needs and doing whatever it takes to keep her safe."

She fidgeted in her seat. "I'm happy to volunteer to provide extra security. I've had some experience with bodyguard assignments."

Quinn shook his head. "A bodyguard isn't good enough. Fiona's only three. It's not like a stranger can tell her to keep her head down and expect her to comply, or reason with her. She needs someone she trusts, someone she'll bond with. I don't want the split second it takes one of my security men to react or get her attention to be the split second that gets her killed." Quinn stood, emphasizing his point and ending the conversation. "She needs a nanny."

Miranda stood to boldly match his stance. "Then she needs someone besides me. I'm not good with kids. I've never had any experience with them."

Bravo for Michael Cutler's diplomacy. He stood, as well, diffusing the tension radiating off Miranda. "Then how do you know you're not good with them?"

Quinn followed up on the logic of Michael's lead. "I don't have time to take one of my bodyguards and teach him how not to frighten my little girl. Nor do I have time to train a nanny with the skills you already possess."

Her proud shoulders sagged for a moment, then stiffened again. "All right, Mr. Gallagher. You have yourself a nanny. I need to go home and pack some gear." She turned to Michael. "I'm assuming I can use my police-issue equipment and weaponry?"

Michael nodded. "And I've got SWAT Team 1 on call to back you up if you need anything."

"Thank you, sir." She gathered her gloves and stocking cap off the desk and reached for her coat on the back of her chair. "When I get back I'd like to meet whatever security you have on staff so I can learn their names, recognize faces, get a handle on procedure here. I'll want a tour of the entire estate, as well. I don't want any hidden gates or staff-only entrances to surprise me. I'll need pass codes or keys to whatever type of physical locks you have on the place."

"I'll make the arrangements." Quinn picked up the phone to call David again. "I'd like you back here by seven. Fiona's bedtime is at eight, and that's strictly observed—even on holidays. Maybe especially on holidays with all the excitement. It's important to maintain her routine."

Miranda nodded, then pulled her black cap on, camouflaging the femininity of her beautiful hair. "I'll see myself out. Make sure security locks up after me."

She paused to look at Fiona, lying on her belly with a water marker and drawing mat, with something like disbelief or even dread on her face. Then she shook it off and hurried into the hallway toward the front door.

"Michael..." Quinn's heart squeezed in his chest as he watched Fiona arrange her doll beside her and tuck another marker beneath the stuffed hand so that they could draw together. There'd be a hell of a price to pay once he found out who had threatened to take that precious life away from him. "You're certain Officer Murdock is capable of being a nanny to Fiona?"

Michael was a wise man who knew how to choose his words well. "She'll keep your daughter safe."

Chapter Four

Something wasn't right.

Miranda doused her headlights and climbed out of her truck as soon as she was through the front gates of the Gallagher estate. Pulling her stocking cap low around her ears, she tucked her ponytail into the back of her navy blue coat so that there was nothing to reflect in the lights from the flood lamps mounted over the security cameras there. With a bit of nimble timing, she slipped through the gates before they clanged shut and locked behind her, and she slipped into the shadows of the moonless night.

She stopped behind a towering pin oak to peer up and down the line of walls and ivy. The car was back. Well, *a* black sedan was parked against the sidewalk about an eighth of a mile from the gate. Without proper streetlamps out here, it was impossible to make out if it was the same car from this afternoon.

And where was the guard? Hadn't Quinn Gallagher ordered his security chief to place a man at the front entrance?

If so, where was he? She'd come in exactly the same

way she had that afternoon, punching a button and being cleared over the intercom system. Even though she was now technically a member of the household staff, someone should have stopped her.

She inhaled deeply, then slowly released her breath so that she didn't create a telltale cloud in the cold air that might reveal her presence. Calming her pulse rate the way she had at the shooting range last night, Miranda reached up beneath her coat and pulled her gun from the holster clipped inside the back of her dark jeans.

Rule 1 of SWAT was reconnaissance. Know your enemy. Know his location. Know his intention. Action was pointless unless you had a plan.

Of course, she'd been checking out a similar hunch about suspicious activity that day the Rich Girl Killer had clocked her in the head and left her for dead so that he could go after his real target. She'd been so intent on proving her worth and saving the day that she hadn't seen him coming until it was too late to use her weapon, too late to get the jump on him. She'd fought him off, but she was so woozy from the initial blow that she passed out before she could stop him. She'd failed.

Tonight there were some niggling doubts that she could handle this similar situation on her own. But without Captain Cutler, Sergeant Delgado and the others, she was a team of one. She didn't have the luxury of second-guessing herself. Michael Cutler and Quinn Gallagher were counting on her to do this job. Time to get some answers.

Sticking close to the trees, she crept several yards

through the snow, past the parked car. Crouching low, she raised her Glock between two steady hands and approached the car from the rear blind spot. Jeans or not, she still wore her service boots. The composite soles had picked up some melt-away salt and now she was crunching across the cleared pavement.

But she could hear the radio music rocking out from here. No way could they hear her approach. She could make out two silhouettes inside—the driver and a passenger in the front seat. Not the same setup as before. But if one of them had silver hair, then they had a lot of questions to answer.

"KCPD! Open up! Get out of the car. Get out of the car now!" She slipped her fingers beneath the passenger-side handle and lifted, quickly returning her grip to the Glock. "Hands on your head. Get out!"

The sudden blare of music faded into background noise in her head. "What the hell…?"

Both men were wearing GSS Security uniform jackets. And both were slumped in their seats.

Miranda quickly shucked a glove and pressed her fingers against the side of the passenger's neck. He had a pulse, faint but steady.

She leaned in to turn off the radio and shut down the engine. As she reached across, she took note of the coffee spilled across the driver's lap, and of the cup tipped over in the passenger's lax fingers and dripping onto the floor mat at his feet.

Surging adrenaline sparked through Miranda's senses. The guards had been drugged. Why? She glanced up at the gates. The man in the command center had spoken to her before *un*locking the gates. Was the danger already inside? Were the Gallaghers under attack?

Ah, hell. Her team of one suddenly seemed awfully small and outnumbered. She needed to get help. She needed to sound the alarm.

"Hey!" She shook the man closest to her. Dark hair. The driver was a blond. Neither had been the man watching the estate earlier today. She lightly smacked his cheek. "Wake up!"

He groaned and leaned back, his head lolling against the headrest. But he didn't wake up. Glancing up and down the street, she saw no sign of anything. No vehicle. No pedestrians. No lights beyond the holiday decorations adorning a couple of the neighboring driveways. Isolated. Alone. Again.

Her breath came hard and fast in her chest. She hadn't seen anyone when the RGK had blindsided her, either. No, no, no. She couldn't let those self-doubts get inside her head.

Miranda's toes danced inside her boots. Treat this like she was on the firing range. Take control. "Think, Murdock. Think."

She tried to wake the driver, but both men were out for the count. Her instinct was to reach for the radio on her shoulder and call in backup. Only, her hand tapped nothing but wool. She was in her civvies now. She had her cell phone in her pocket. But did she call 911 or Captain Cutler? She had no clue about Quinn Gallagher's number or his chief of security or...

Her gaze alighted on the dashboard radio. Of course. They'd be connected to the estate's security office.

But as she pushed the snoozing driver aside to get to the radio, something tumbled from the inside of his coat and landed at her feet. "What's this?"

She picked it up.

The damp wind whipped at her cheeks, but she was turning cold from the inside out.

It was a little doll. A roughly made, voodoolike miniature of the rag doll Fiona Gallagher always had with her. Only this one was covered in something red and sticky. And instead of beautifully embroidered eyes, this one had two tiny slashes drawn across its face.

A dead doll.

Miranda pulled out a piece of paper that had been tucked inside the doll's dress. She unrolled the stained note and read the message typed inside.

And then the anger kicked in, casting out self-doubts and second-guessing.

See how easily I can get to you? Make it right, Gallagher, or this is your little girl.

Uh-uh. Not on Miranda Murdock's watch.

She put the note back where she'd found it and pushed the drugged driver aside to grab the radio. She had no idea about GSS procedures, so as soon as she had a clear channel and a stern "Who is this?" she went with the whole get-your-butt-out-here-now protocol.

"Hey, whoever's in the command center, this is Randy Murdock, KCPD. I'm one of you now, and I need backup. You've got a situation with your guards here at the front gate. Someone in charge will want to see this. Oh, and you may want to call an ambulance."

"WHATEVER THEY SPIKED the coffee with will have to wait until we can get it to a lab," Quinn declared. "But this is gelatin. Red gelatin and food coloring." He tossed his plastic gloves into the trash can beside his desk—resisting the urge to toss the gruesome doll in there, as well. "Probably made with corn syrup instead of water to keep it from setting completely. It's an old kid's trick to make fake blood."

"This isn't any kid's joke." Miranda stopped her pacing on the far side of his desk and came up between his security chief, David Damiani, and her own boss, Michael Cutler. "It's a very calculated, very sick way to make you feel threatened."

"It's working." Quinn's gaze skipped from her slender curves to David's bulk and steaming temper, to Michael's lanky height and piercingly intelligent eyes, and back to the unblinking intensity of Miranda's mossy gaze. Was that concern he saw written there? Temper? Fear?

Beyond his own intellect and drive to succeed, one of the things that had aided Quinn in his rise to the top of his field was his ability to read people. David was ticked off that his men had gotten hurt and that all his preventive measures and training hadn't been able to stop the attack. Michael was thinking, evaluating possible plans of action, trying to come up with a scenario where everyone came out unharmed.

But Miranda? She was a complete mystery to him.

With her gun and plain talk, she was as tough as any man in the room. Yet there was something curiously vulnerable about that tumble of emotions alternately darkening and brightening her eyes. Her blue jeans and plain brown sweater did little to highlight her femininity, yet his body had hummed with a distinctly masculine energy from the moment she'd entered the room—peeling off her stocking cap and shaking that golden ponytail down her back, removing her coat and tossing it onto a chair with that effortlessly sinuous grace of hers.

Miranda Murdock was a baffling conundrum he wanted to figure out.

But analyzing that fascination was a distraction he didn't need right now.

The clock is ticking. The text he'd received while watching Fiona open up her gifts this morning had been perfectly clear.

"The only way an enemy could get under my skin *is* to threaten my daughter." Quinn took his eyes off the distraction in the room and paced off the walls of books surrounding them. "The question is why? Who did I step on? What offense did I commit? I paid the money he wanted."

"Into a Swiss account we're working on tracing," David reported. "Thus far, we've dead-ended at a dummy corporation called United Lithographers of Southern Europe."

"U LOSE?" Miranda's eyes went dark again as she

pieced together the acronym that was a mocking message in itself. "That's cold."

David's expression was almost a sneer as he glanced down at her. "We're still investigating."

"Have you found out where the text messages are coming from?"

The follow-up question didn't improve David's mood. "Disposable cell phones. A different one each time. Impossible to trace."

"Apparently, I've really ticked someone off." Quinn didn't need bickering children in the room right now, each trying to prove he or she was the better security expert. "I spent today updating that old patent of mine, which is still practically worthless on the market, and I sent it to the generic email account specified. Now I have to run a simulation to prove that it works by noon tomorrow. I've got a couple of techs in the GSS lab working to trace it in the meantime." He sank onto a black leather sofa, then shot to his feet again. He wasn't used to being a man without answers. He didn't like it. "What is it I have to 'make right' by the start of the New Year?"

"That could be a long list," Michael suggested. Add guilt to the list of problems Quinn needed to fix. He'd taken his friend from his new wife and baby, and teenage son, on their first Christmas together as a family. But Michael hadn't complained. "You don't become as rich as you are without someone else being jealous of what you have. A competitor might think he got the short end of a business deal. You fired an employee who feels he or she didn't deserve it. Someone thinks you took credit for an invention he or she worked on."

"I didn't," Quinn argued. "I came from nothing. I worked hard and used my brains to earn every last penny I have."

Michael shrugged. "This perp we're looking for doesn't have to think logically, the way you do, Quinn. He may be fueled by emotions and misconceptions. What matters is that, in his mind—or hers—you've done him wrong."

"So this guy could just be some lunatic?" Nobody in the room argued the possibility. Quinn raked his fingers through his hair. "Ah, hell."

"Could it be something personal?" David asked.

Quinn stopped at the mantel over the empty fireplace and studied the collection of family pictures there. Growing up, he and his mother had had so little. Now he had so much. But none of it mattered. Only one thing mattered. "I have no personal life beyond Fiona."

"What about Valeska?"

Quinn's gaze snapped across the room to David's dark eyes at the mention of his late wife. "Val worked her way up through my company. She earned her vice presidency before I ever married her. If somebody resents that…"

David averted his gaze for a moment, knowing he'd hit a hot button. But Quinn hadn't hired the former military man because he shied away from a potential confrontation. The GSS security chief crossed the study to meet him at the fireplace. "What about Valeska's father? Vasily Gordeeva? He spent a lot of years in that political prison. Supposedly, the U.S. was supposed to be a safe place for his family. Does he blame you for Valeska's murder?"

"Three years after the fact?" Tilting his head to the ceiling, Quinn vented his frustration on a sigh before answering. "The Rich Girl Killer murdered my wife in the backyard of our own house that day—leaving my infant daughter in the stroller right beside her. And this bastard thinks I need to pay a higher price than that?"

Miranda's soft gasp reminded him that not everyone knew the story as well as he did. She turned away when he tried to meet her stricken stare and apologize for his bluntness. But he could flush the anger and grief from his voice. That was a skill he'd learned long ago, back with the bullies in the Shoemaker Trailer Court. "I've never even met my father-in-law. Val grew up here in the States without him. Even when I did business in St. Feodor, she never went there. It wasn't safe for her to return to the country. How could Vasily hold me responsible for her murder if the two of them never had a relationship? And now the plant in St. Feodor is closed. Other than a few investors there—who made a tidy profit through GSS, I might add—I have no ties."

He was surprisingly relieved to see Miranda face him again. "Your father-in-law is in prison?"

"In the Eastern European country of Lukinburg." Quinn scratched his fingers through his hair and moved back toward his desk. "He's a political dissident, accused of financing a failed rebellion there. I don't know much more of the story than that. For their own protection, he severed his relationship to Valeska and her mother, and they emigrated to the U.S. She never talked about him."

"That sounds like heavy stuff."

"We're talking about *my* enemies here, Miranda. Not Vasily Gordeeva's. This enemy is right here at home."

"With all due respect, sir, we don't know where your enemy is."

Why was she arguing this? "This isn't about politics in a foreign country. This is about greed or payback or both." Quinn stopped and turned right in front of her. "I'm guessing I'll receive another task to complete tomorrow—something every day until the end of the year. Let's try to get some answers sooner rather than later, shall we?"

She propped her hands at her hips and tilted her eyes up to his. "Well, I think you're asking the wrong question."

He opened his mouth to reply to the provocative taunt, but for once in his life, the right words wouldn't come to him. He had to move away before he could speak again. "Michael, isn't there some chain of command you teach your people to follow?"

"I also teach them to think on their feet." Not a yes man in the room tonight. "What is it, Randy?"

Her cheeks heated with color and her expression animated at her captain's encouragement to share her opinion. "Why drug the guards? Why not kill them outright? They didn't hesitate to kill those men at the plant overseas. If you're going to take the risk of them being able to identify you, why give them the chance to wake up and point a finger?"

Sound reasoning. Hell, why hadn't he thought of that? More irritatingly, Quinn wondered why he hadn't expected that from her. Why couldn't he get a read on Miranda Murdock? She was antagonistic yet insecure. She was a physical woman, yet she also showed a keen intellect.

Michael, fortunately, wasn't wasting any time of the puzzle of Miranda Murdock. "So whoever served them that coffee is either someone they know and trust, or it was done by someone they never saw at all."

David thundered back across the room. "If you're suggesting that one of my men is behind this—"

"Check them out," Quinn ordered.

"—after I've personally and thoroughly screened every last one of them."

Damn it, this was *his* company, *his* family that was being threatened. He paid Damiani a lot of money to follow his commands. "Screen them again."

Michael was a little more diplomatic. "It'd narrow down our list of suspects. Your men were drugged outside the gate because the perp couldn't get inside. Security's still good here."

No wonder he was one of KCPD's top negotiators. A deep breath heaved through David's barrel chest and his burst of defensive temper dissipated. "But if they can figure out how to get to them out there, it's only a matter of time before they figure out how to get past my men and the protocols here. I'd better not have a mole on my team."

"Let's change up the protocols," Quinn suggested, thankful that someone in the room could keep his head.

"I want your best men on this, David. And find out who the hell drugged those guards."

"Daddy?" A soft voice from the hallway turned all four adults toward the open door. Fiona hugged her doll against her chest, her blue eyes wide as they sought out Quinn's. "Why you angwy?"

Quinn glared at the guard lurking behind her in the hallway. A grown man couldn't keep a little girl in her room for an hour?

"She insisted we come down here," the man apologized.

Condemning his own raised voice, Quinn dismissed the guard and scooped Fiona up into his arms, turning her so she wouldn't get a glimpse of the mutilated doll on his desk. "What are you doing here, sweetie? I thought you were watching the new movie Santa brought you up in your room."

Her small fingers splayed across his cheek. "Petwa wants more cookies."

Quinn shifted his gaze to the fraying embroidery of the doll's blue eyes. "I think Petra has had enough sweets for one day." He pressed a kiss against the delicate fingers on his cheek. "So have you, young lady."

Her tiny mouth stretched with a yawn and Quinn checked his watch. As much as he loved the sweet weight of her in his arms, he had work to do. Above anything else, it was his job to protect her. And that required changing security codes and talking revised strategies with David Damiani and Michael.

So he handed Fiona over to the new nanny. "It's after seven now. It's time to get Fiona to bed."

"Wha—?" Quinn held on a moment longer, worried for a moment that she wasn't even going to wrap her arms around his daughter. "But we haven't finished debriefing. What's our next plan of action? I won't know the new security protocols. I don't know the old ones yet." Miranda's hands finally closed around Fiona's back and thigh, and she shifted her onto one hip. "I don't even know where her bedroom is."

Miranda's eyes were dark like a pine forest now, yet wide with panic. The woman should never play poker. Definitely a puzzle.

"Fiona can show you."

Given a mission to do, Fiona sat up straight, excitement chasing away her fatigue. "I know." She squiggled down to the floor, catching Miranda's hand along the way. "Come on."

Quinn exchanged a glance with Miranda as Fiona led her out of the room. *Do your job,* he warned silently.

If he wasn't mistaken, Miranda's arched brow read something like *What do you think I've been doing?* Or maybe it was *Help!* as she disappeared around the corner.

The need to go after them, to make sure his decision to hire Miranda to protect his daughter wasn't a mistake, jolted through his legs. But what harm could come to a three-year-old and an armed SWAT cop going upstairs to Fiona's bedroom?

Ignoring the tension that refused to go away, Quinn forced himself to return to the two men at his desk. "Do we have any leads at all on who took out the guards and left this vile message?"

David shook his head. "Holmes and Rowley couldn't have been out for too long because they made their thirty-minute check-in."

"Increase it to fifteen-minute reports. Go through the security camera footage to find out when they got that coffee, if they stopped anyone at the gate, or if anyone walked up to the car." Quinn pulled off his glasses to rub at his tired eyes. "We need to find out who's behind this. First, a foreign base of operation. Then the GSS offices here in KC. Now my home. He's getting way too close for my comfort."

"Permission to speak freely, sir?"

Quinn put his glasses back on to bring the security chief into focus. "Of course."

"I know your judgment is a little skewed right now with the threat against Fiona." David thumbed over his shoulder toward the empty doorway. "But Dirty Harriet there is a loose cannon. She pulled a gun on my men."

"They were unconscious."

"What if they weren't? We'd have had a fire fight in the middle of the street on Christmas night." He pulled back the front of his jacket to prop his hands near the holster at his waist. "Do you really want someone like that around your daughter?"

"Considering *she* detected the threat against this home when your men couldn't, yes."

Chapter Five

"Is that choking you, sweetie?" Miranda frowned at the neckline of the long pink underwear-looking pajamas she'd put on Fiona as she tucked the quilt around her in the canopy bed. She'd spent too much time familiarizing herself with the layout of the bedroom suite, complete with retractable steel window shields and a panic room she could access inside the walk-in closet. She should have given a little more thought to pajama etiquette. "Maybe they snap in the front." She tossed the covers back and smiled an apology to the little girl. "Will you stand up for me?"

They ought to put directions on these things for first-timers like her. But Fiona was more than happy to jump to her feet on the bed. She weighed next to nothing as she braced a hand on Miranda's shoulder and dutifully picked up each foot so that she could turn the pajamas around and get them back on the right way.

Miranda fastened the last snap up beneath the girl's chin and slid her fingers inside the neckline to make sure they fit more comfortably this time. "All righty. Down you go."

With a giggle that made Miranda smile, Fiona plopped down on her bottom and then leaned back into the pillows.

"Good night, Fiona."

But a small hand grabbed the cover before she could pull it up to her young charge's chin. The quizzical narrowing of Fiona's round blue eyes reminded Miranda of another Gallagher who seemed to find fault with a lot of the things she said or did. "We didn't bwush my teeth."

"Oh." Duh. Even though she wasn't familiar with the needs of three-year-old girls, at the very least Miranda should have been thinking about her own nighttime routine. "We'd better go take care of that. We don't want all your teeth to fall out of your head."

The joke must have needed an older audience.

Miranda shrugged off the confused response and kept smiling.

"Show me where you keep your toothbrush."

Using one of the posts at the foot of the bed, Fiona climbed over the safety railing to the floor, then reached back for that ever-present doll. With "Petra" in one hand, and Miranda's fingers in the other, Fiona led her into the connecting bathroom.

It was almost a reversal of roles as Fiona showed Miranda each step of her routine. First, she climbed onto a stool just inside the bathroom to turn on the light. Then there was another step stool in front of the sink. There, she filled a plastic cup with water and wet the brush herself before squeezing a fistful of toothpaste onto the bristles. Miranda arched an eyebrow at her reflection in the mirror over the sink. She was on a steep learn-ing curve here. *Pj's close in front. Prep the toothbrush for her. Watch out where and how high this one climbs.*

After the task was done, and Miranda had wiped away the extra foam from Fiona's face and hands and the countertop, she tried putting her to bed again. Pa-jamas on the right way. Teeth brushed. Doll and girl tucked in. Head for the light switch. She'd already spot-ted the night-light in the plug beside the bathroom door, but she knew some children had a fear of the darkness. So she paused a moment to ask, "Is it okay if I turn the big light off?"

The blue eyes blinked, but never looked away.

"What?"

"What about my stowy?"

"You like a bedtime story?"

Fiona beamed with a smile and nodded.

Miranda located the white bookshelf nestled between the windows overlooking the second-story porch and crossed to it. Picture books. Beginning readers. Clas-sic chapter books. Alphabet books. *Overload.* "What do you like to read?"

Fiona giggled again. "I can't wead."

"No, I mean, what do you want me to...?" That laugh was a delightfully musical sound. Maybe the jokes all had to do with her own incompetence in the bedtime arena, but Fiona's giggle went a long way toward easing Miranda's fears that she was going to warp the child for life as long as she was in charge of her care. "What shall *we* read this evening?"

"The pink pwincess one."

It took a search through five different princess

books to find the right adventure Fiona was looking for. "Okay. Here we go."

Miranda started the story in the rocking chair beside the bed. But two pages in and Fiona was up on her knees with the covers thrown back, twirling around like the princess in her ball gown. By page five, they were both growling like the dragon who wanted to eat all the flowers in the kingdom.

Miranda was on her feet, playing the part of the prince, dueling the bedpost with a toy broomstick sword while Fiona giggled and roared away, when she realized there was another presence in the room. A tall, bespectacled, steely-eyed presence filling the doorway. As much as Fiona's laugh delighted, Quinn Gallagher's scowl sobered her up.

"Uh-oh." Miranda stopped mid–dragon growl and tossed the chubby-handled broom back into the toy chest before closing the book with her finger marking the place. She wished she didn't feel quite so much like a little girl who'd been caught making too much noise at a slumber party. She hugged the book to her chest, subconsciously turning it into a shield between her and Quinn. "Fiona said she needed a story."

"A story, yes. Not a live reenactment."

"We were using our imaginations and having a little silly fun. You do allow your daughter to have fun, don't you?"

He stood with his arms crossed over his chest, the corded strength of his forearms straining beneath the rolled-up sleeves of his button-down shirt. No, perhaps he was a man who didn't do *silly*. "Her bedtime routine is supposed to be a quiet time to help her relax and go to sleep."

Lois Lane had it all wrong. Clark Kent was the hottie. Or maybe Miranda was the one who was all wrong. *Get it together, Murdock.* It must be the late hour, or those extra lonesome working-on-a-holiday genes, kicking in. She was here to protect this family, here to do a favor for the captain. Lusting after her cranky boss wasn't part of the job description.

She exhaled a sigh of frustration and returned the book to the bookshelf. "I told you I wasn't any good at this."

"Let's go, sweetie." Quinn picked up Fiona and smoothed the dark curls off her flushed face before laying her in the bed and pulling up the covers. "Daddy will tuck you in."

"The dwagon goes *grrrr,*" Fiona roared with high-pitched enthusiasm, curling her fingers into a little claw the way Miranda had. "And the pwince and pwincess... e-yah, e-yah." She thrust out her fist into Quinn's chest, mimicking Miranda's rebel charge perfectly.

"I'll 'e-yah' you, young lady." Quinn caught her little fist and kissed it before tucking it under the cover, as well. "And the dragon and the prince and princess became friends and planted a garden and lived happily ever after."

"Wandy tells it better."

"Maybe that's a story you should read during play-time, not when it's bedtime."

"I'm not sleepy..." Fiona's big yawn was Miranda's cue to exit. Fiona turned her face into the soft cotton of her doll. "'Night, Daddy. 'Night, Wandy."

Being included in the three-year-old's goodbye warmed Miranda like a gentle squeeze of her hand, chasing away some of the loneliness and inadequacy she'd been feeling. "Good night, Fiona."

Miranda was in the hallway, almost to her room next door, when a real hand snagged her wrist. Instinctively, she twisted free and spun around to face her opponent. But she had no place to go when Quinn closed in on her. She had to flatten her back against the wall and stay put, ignoring the poke of her gun and holster at her waist. Either that, or she could shove her boss's best friend in the chest or disable him in some other, considerably more painful, way. Miranda opted for standing tall and staying put.

Quinn braced his hand on the wall beside her head and leaned in. "I do not need you to question me in front of my people. Or my daughter. We have routines in this household for a reason."

"Control freak much?"

"You're the damn nanny. Not my conscience. I need you to do what I say when I say it."

Their voices were charged, hushed, intimate, as they kept their argument beyond the earshot of anyone else in the house. "I'm here to protect your daughter, not to be bullied by you."

"Bullied?"

"You have all the money, all the power—you're used to people jumping to do your bidding." His eyes were blue, blue, blue, up close like this. Even the refraction of his lenses couldn't distort their color. Miranda felt like a specimen under a microscope as they evaluated every nuance of her words and expression. "Maybe that's how this crazy countdown to New Year's got inside all your state-of-the-art security—because *you* haven't thought of every possible threat. Smart as you are, Mr. Gallagher, you don't know everything."

"Are you always this much trouble, Officer Murdock?"

"Pretty much."

They weren't touching, but they were both breathing hard as the furtive exchange of tempers and opinions mutated into a different kind of heat. Their breaths mingled and their chests nearly brushed against each other with every inhale. Her head filled with the spicy scent of shaving cream or soap on his skin. Her body warmed with the proximity of his body lined up with hers. She wasn't even aware of the holster poking into her backside anymore. Quinn's gaze fixated on her lips, and Miranda couldn't look away from those laser-blue eyes.

This was crazy. *She* was crazy. She was the bodyguard and he was the boss and they butted heads, and she really shouldn't be wondering what it would be like if he kissed her right now.

She wrapped her fingers around the chair rail on the wall behind her to conquer the urge to brush that stray lock of hair off his forehead. But she couldn't. She shouldn't. Finally, in a breathy voice, she summoned the will to whisper, "You're in my personal space."

"I am." There was something bold and sexy about the statement of fact and the idea that he must be feeling this, too, or he would have retreated by now. "I don't get you, Miranda."

"I *am* a little different from the average woman," she conceded wryly.

It was the opening those niggling self-doubts needed to sneak inside her head. But when she lowered her gaze and looked away, Quinn's hand was there, gently pinching her chin between his thumb and forefinger and tilting her face back up to his. "One way or another, I'm going to figure you out."

It sounded like a vow.

Any sensible reply lodged in her throat. As little as she knew about raising little girls, she knew even less about healthy romantic relationships with grown men.

Fortunately, she was granted a reprieve from those shortcomings piling on the growing confusion inside her.

"Daddy?" a soft voice called from the bedroom.

Just like that, Quinn's touch was gone. He took his uniquely masculine scent with him as he shoved his fingers through his already mussed hair and put the width of the hallway between them.

"That shouldn't have happened."

Miranda hugged her arms around her middle, feeling strangely chilled. "Nothing did."

Technically, that was true.

Quinn's jerky nod indicated that he didn't quite believe that a sensual awareness hadn't just erupted and continued to simmer between them, either. But she understood the signs of dismissal in his posture, and the need to return to the business at hand.

"I'll sit with Fiona for a few minutes and get her settled. David Damiani and the guards on duty at the house this evening are gathered in the command center to meet with you. He'll get you a card for the electronic locks and explain the pass codes, panic rooms and security lockdown procedure." Fiona called out again, and Quinn moved toward his daughter's door. "The command center is down on the basement level. I'll join you as soon as she's asleep."

"Quinn?"

"Please. Do not argue with me this one time."

"I was just going to say that I'll do better with Fiona. I can get online tonight, or go to the library tomorrow. There have to be some tips and tricks somewhere to teach me how to do the nanny gig."

His eyes narrowed into that quizzical frown. "You're doing just fine. I haven't heard that kind of laughter from her for a long time. I'm the idiot who's being too critical of too many things right now. I'm just…" His broad shoulders rose and fell with a weary sigh, letting her know that she wasn't the only one plagued by self-doubt in this house. "I want to know who the hell has the nerve to threaten my daughter."

"We'll find him," Miranda promised. Although whether she was talking as a cop or a woman, she wasn't sure. She checked her gun at her back and offered Quinn a smile. "Captain Cutler always says we have to trust the team. So let us all do our jobs. No one is going to hurt Fiona. Not on my watch."

Miranda just prayed that, for this overwhelmed father and his sweet little girl, she wasn't the member of the team who let everyone down. Again.

THE IMAGE OF THE BLOND-HAIRED woman in the black uniform on the computer screen went dark at the punch of a button.

This was an interesting new development. Imagine GSS, a global force in personal security technology, bringing in outside help to keep its own CEO and his daughter safe. It was ironic, really. So the king of Gallagher Security Systems was feeling *insecure*.

That was satisfaction to take to the bank.

Of course, having the woman on the premises would make it a little harder to get to Fiona Gallagher. But it wouldn't be impossible, not by a long shot. It simply meant adding one more tally to the body count.

A trail of dead bodies, from the Kalahari Desert to Kansas City, Missouri, would certainly put a crimp in the almighty Quinn Gallagher's sterling reputation. If the man behind GSS couldn't keep his own people safe, then why would anyone trust his company to protect them? He'd be ruined.

It was something worth smiling about.

Taking his daughter would destroy him. She was the only thing meaningful enough to Quinn Gallagher to ultimately be worth taking. It was the only thing meaningful enough to count as payback for what Quinn Gallagher had done.

Gallagher had exacted too great a price on his way to the top of his field. Hearts had been broken, dreams shattered. He hadn't protected everyone who should have mattered. An unjust price had been paid for his success. It was time to take back a little—make that *all*—of what he owed.

The boss leaned back in the office chair and placed a call to the man who'd required the tidy sum of two and a half million dollars for his team to carry out the necessary work for the rest of the week. Two and a half million was chicken feed to a man like Quinn Gallagher. Imagine how much would be taken from him by the time this was all said and done.

A split second passed before the man answered. "Yes?"

"Is everything in place?" His hesitation wasn't the best way to begin a report. The boss demanded an explanation. "What is it?"

"We couldn't get the doll placed where you wanted it, but Gallagher has it now."

Good enough. The bloody doll had been more about shock and diversion and making Gallagher squirm. Quinn Gallagher thought he was smart enough to plan for every contingency. But there was one he would never see coming. "And the other?"

"Soon. You were right. My guy piggybacked right off Gallagher's design file when he emailed it to us." First his business, then his family. Step by step, Gallagher would go down. "As soon as he starts running the software simulation, we'll have access to the entire computer system. Once we're in, the building will be ours. You can deliver the next message whenever you're ready."

"Good." Time to initiate the next phase of the plan.

Chapter Six

5 days until Midnight, New Year's Eve

"Hey, John. Sorry to get you up so early." Miranda beamed inside and out at the gritty image of her brother in his desert camouflage uniform on the screen of her laptop. "Merry Christmas, big guy."

"Merry Christmas, kiddo. Sorry to keep you up so late."

"That's okay. I'm on duty, anyway."

"In your pajamas? Where's your gun stashed?"

Miranda curled her legs beneath her in the chair in the Gallagher estate's security command center and grinned. At least one perk to working the holidays for a man who was as wealthy and techno-savvy as he was unsettling and opinionated was access to a pretty sophisticated computer setup. This was the best satellite link she'd had with her brother since he'd been deployed. "Long story. So tell me, what did you do to celebrate?"

John's hair was a few shades darker than her blond locks, but the same green eyes looked back at her and smiled. "Well, I just stuffed my belly with a ridiculous amount of food. They went all out for the holiday meal—ham, turkey, prime rib. Baked potatoes. Mashed potatoes. Sweet potatoes. Cherry pie. Pecan pie. Chocolate cake. Ice cream..."

"Stop. I'm gaining weight just listening to all that." Although his deep, indulgent tone was familiar, she couldn't help but notice the tight lines bracketing his smile. "You look tired."

"I just came off the front line today."

The time difference between the States and the Middle Eastern region where his marine unit was stationed required these rare face-to-face hookups to take place at odd hours. But she didn't think a lack of sleep fully accounted for the gaunt look of his handsome face. "John? You do remember that I'm a twenty-eight-year-old grown-up now, right? You don't have to protect me the way you used to. Did something happen?"

He looked away from the camera for a second, then tried a little harder to make his smile stick. "Did I tell you I got that care package you sent? Loved the books and the sports drinks. Not sure what I'm going to do with the red-and-green socks, though."

"Nice dodge, big brother." John Murdock avoiding a straight answer raised her concern another notch. "But you didn't answer my question. Is it really that horrible there?"

She and John had been a family unto themselves since the time she'd been a teen and he'd been in his early twenties and their parents had died in a car accident. She could read her brother's moods and expressions like he could read hers—and they didn't keep secrets from each other.

"I'm in a war zone, kiddo. It's rough."

"John…"

His tension eased on a wry laugh. "Fine. I was never able to outlast your stubborn streak." Miranda's heart squeezed in her chest at the pain that passed over his features. "We had a bad encounter on one of our last sorties. I lost a good friend. I asked the CO if I could write a letter to his family. It was tough."

"Oh, John. I'm so sorry." His pain became her own. She was so far away, so helpless to do anything for him. Was there any job she was going to be able to successfully accomplish anymore? *No. Don't go there.* This wasn't about her. She swiped at the tears stinging her eyes and smiled for his benefit. "What can I do to help?"

"Give me a present," John answered, the shift of his wide shoulders making the effort to lighten the mood. "Tell me what you did to celebrate the holiday."

"I worked."

"That's a lousy present. I'm going to have to have a talk with your captain when I get home. At least tell me you have fun plans for New Year's Eve."

"As far as I know, I'm working then, too."

John shook his head. "Can't the criminals let you celebrate at least one holiday?"

"I'm trying to earn some brownie points with Captain Cutler. So I volunteered for a special assignment with one of his friends, Quinn Gallagher." She gestured to the wall of computer towers, wires and monitors behind her. "That's why we've got such a great link this time. Mr. Gallagher is letting me use the computer lab in his security offices."

"That explains why it looks like you're sitting in a bunker. You've got plenty of ventilation there, right?"

"There's a huge cooling system here with all these electronics." She glanced up. "I'm staring at a vent now that leads up to the main floor and is bigger than my closet."

"Maybe I should be there instead of this tent."

"I wish you were. It's hard to feel like celebrating the holidays without you." Miranda patted the belly of her red plaid flannel pants and pouted. "There was no one to bake me a caramel apple pie."

John laughed. It was a good sound to hear, and eased her worry about him just a bit. "You're really roughing it, aren't you?"

"Hey, you haven't had to butt heads with Quinn Gallagher." Her body tingled at the memory of that heated encounter in the upstairs hallway. She hugged her knees up to her chest, trying to dispel the prickly aftershocks of sexual awareness before her brother picked up on any of her unplanned and inappropriate fascination with her temporary boss. "He's like something out of a comic book—a driven, brainiac, his-way-or-the-highway kind of a guy. Although, I haven't decided whether he's more the hero or the villain yet."

"A comic-book character?" John scoffed. "I knew I should have gotten you to read more Austen and Brontë than that fantasy adventure stuff you ate up in school.

You're talking about the guy who created Gallagher Security Systems, right?"

"You've heard of him?"

John thumbed the collar of his captain's uniform. "GSS doesn't make flak vests just for cops."

"I can imagine his company making only the best for our troops. Even his house here in Kansas City is a fortress. I've had a crash course in keyless remotes, motion-activated sensors, panic room protocols and redundant armor systems to close off windows and doors in the event of an attack. I swear, if there's a security technology out there, Quinn Gallagher has it installed here. The whole estate is like a model home for security technology."

"So what are you doing for GSS?"

"It's for Quinn, specifically. There have been threats against the family, and he has this adorable little girl." Who, despite Miranda's screwed-up efforts thus far, seemed to like her, as well. "I'm working as a nanny for a week."

John snorted a laugh. "You? I never pictured you as the domestic type. This Gallagher does know you can't cook, and you've never changed a diaper, or—"

"Give it a rest," she chided with a grin. "I'm the girl's bodyguard. I tried to tell Quinn that we weren't playing to my strengths here. But I met the most important requirement."

"What's that?"

"I was available."

John's deep-voiced chuckle made Miranda smile, as well. "Is there a mother in the picture?"

"Quinn's a widower. Why?"

"Because you've mentioned him by name at least three times in the past thirty seconds. Somebody's got a crush."

Despite the refrigerated temperature of the basement office, Miranda felt her cheeks heat with embarrassment. "I do not. I mean, can you imagine someone like me together with someone like him? There are so many reasons why it would never—"

John's image disappeared off the screen and an odd image blipped into its place. Long tables. Equipment, knobs, wires. A blurry glimpse of a figure whose face was above the angle of the camera shot. There was no marine, no khaki tent wall in the background. For one second, maybe two, she was looking at a different place, a different person.

Miranda's mouth was still open, midprotest, when snowy static blurred the picture on the screen and John suddenly reappeared.

"John?"

"Did we lose the connection?" he asked. "We were supposed to have the feed for twenty minutes."

She unwound her legs and dropped her feet to the floor. "You saw it, too?"

He was sitting up straighter, too. "I lost the signal for a few seconds. Instead of looking at you, I was looking at—" he shrugged "—someplace else."

"Like a visual party line. I don't know what it was."

"Who knows how many satellites we're bouncing off of to make this connection? A line's bound to cross somewhere."

"Yeah." But wouldn't the monitor just go blank or fuzzy if they lost the satellite connection? "I need to go report this."

"Randy?"

"A lot of weird things have been happening here." It had been the weird behavior of a suspect near the witness SWAT Team 1 had been assigned to protect that had diverted her focus, allowing the Rich Girl Killer to sneak up from behind and attack her. Was this a diversion that could take her attention away from protecting Fiona Gallagher? "Do you remember me telling you about the RGK?"

"Yeah. He cracked your head open and you think that means you failed your team. The guy's dead, Randy. He's got nothing to do with a computer glitch."

"I know." Maybe she could confess to her brother the secret self-doubts the police psychologist had had to pry from her. "But I nearly blew that mission to hell, John. And now I second-guess everything. Every thought, every action. Everything I see. I can't let anything happen to that little girl. But I don't know that I'm the best person for this job."

"Nobody trains harder than you. Nobody understands responsibility and wanting to do the right thing more than you. You're smart. You've got good instincts. Hell, I taught you everything I know about staying safe." And he'd done it very well. "I'm the one fighting a war. I do not want to get a telegram that says something happened to my baby sister while I was away."

Her heart lurched in her chest. "Thanks for the pep talk. I'll be careful if you will."

"Deal."

"Swear?"

"I swear." He nodded toward her. "Now trust those instincts and go find out what just happened here."

They each touched their hands to their respective screens. It was as close to a hug as either one of them was going to get. "I love you, John."

"I love you, too, sis."

Miranda's fingers were still there when the satellite feed ended and the monitor returned to its screensaver image.

And then she was on her feet, searching for anyone else on the estate who was still up at this hour.

"WHAT ARE YOU DOING OUT here?" Miranda's footsteps had been noiseless on the stairs, and yet Quinn had known he was no longer alone the moment she reached the landing. Some switch of hyperawareness had been turned on in his brain, specifically tuning his radar to alert to her presence. "Is something wrong?"

He pulled back from the door frame where he'd been watching Fiona sleep and quietly closed the door to her room.

"Quinn?" She'd come up beside him, the point of her chin tilted toward him, those green eyes sharp with concern as they tried to read his expression.

"She's fine." He tightened his robe around his bare chest and the sweatpants he'd worn to bed. He adjusted his glasses at the temple to buy him another second to wipe the depth of his worry from his face before turning to her. "I'm the one who can't sleep. I keep thinking that if I drop my guard for even one moment, if I let her out of my sight…"

"That's what I'm here for, right?" She pointed to her bedroom door. "I can take the comforter off my bed and bunk on the floor in here if you like. I grew up doing lots of camping with my family, so it's no problem."

Keeping the fact that he'd been tempted to do that very thing to himself, Quinn shook his head. The one person innocently unaware of all the dangers swirling around his daughter was Fiona herself. But if she woke up to find one of them in there with her, that sharp little brain of hers would quickly realize that something was wrong. It was one thing for him to be afraid, but seeing that fear tainting his daughter's eyes would tear him in two. "She'll be fine. Father's prerogative to worry, you know."

"Sounds like my big brother." She gently splayed her fingers against the door. "Fiona's a lucky girl. It's a secure feeling to know someone's looking out for you."

Miranda's serene smile when she spoke of her family eased an answering smile onto his own mouth. "Did you make the connection to your brother?"

She nodded, curling her fingers into her palm. "Thank you." In the dim light of the hallway, Miranda seemed shorter, not quite up to Quinn's nose where she'd been earlier in the evening. A more observant glance up and down the red and white of her pajamas revealed that she'd been running around the estate in her socks, adding a younger, inexplicably vulnerable air to the tough chick who'd been armed and dangerous and argumentative from nearly the first moment they'd met. "Talking to John is the best present I could have asked for."

So why wasn't she still smiling? "But...?"

Her shoulders lifted with a deep breath. "Something hinky happened to the link while I was talking to him. John disappeared for a couple of seconds, and I was looking at something else, some*where* else. Kind of like someone switching the channel on the TV, and then switching it back. I asked the guard on duty, O'Brien, about it. But he seemed to know less about computers than I do."

"Hinky, hmm? Let me check." Her confusion was cause enough to trigger his own concern. And since he wasn't sleeping, anyway, Quinn headed down the stairs to his office study, with Miranda following on quick, silent footsteps. He sat at his desk, turned on a lamp and pulled up the estate's mainframe access, typing in code after code to get into the secure server that constituted the brain for all of the estate's electronic activity.

He felt her lean against the back of the leather chair to look over his shoulder. "You know how to do that?"

"I know my way around lots of different technology. I designed this system myself." Once he was in, he scrolled through all the recent online activity. "I didn't make my millions by being a pretty face."

"No, you couldn't do that."

What? Quinn stopped midtype and turned in his chair to question the taunt.

She slapped her hand over her mouth, her face blushing rosy pink all around at the stray thought she'd spoken out loud. The hand came down and she backed away from the chair. "That didn't come out right. You aren't pretty. Not with the chest and the arms and the… I mean, you've got that whole hero-beneath-the-nerdy-black-glasses thing going for you…" Her hands came forward, imploring him to understand her embarrassed rambling. "You're Clark Kent on the outside. But underneath, you're really…" Her posture withered as she hugged her arms around her waist. "Shutting up now."

Maybe this woman would never make sense to him. Still, Quinn appreciated the roundabout stroke to a male ego that hadn't really cared about such things since his wife's death. So Miranda had noticed something beneath the button-down suits and glasses that had long defined him to the world. Nice to know he wasn't the only one in the room battling a little bit of ill-timed lust.

He grinned as he went back to his search. "I always fancied myself more of a Batman type." The grateful laugh behind him touched something a little deeper than his ego and warmed him inside. Going head-to-head with Miranda Murdock was invigorating, but this quieter, friendlier detente between them was waking parts of him that had been dormant for a long time. "All our computers here are on a server that goes through the mainframe at GSS. I'm just double-checking to see if there was a—"

That shouldn't be there.

Quinn pulled off his glasses and got right up to the monitor to verify what he was seeing. Son of a bitch. So brilliant. So simple.

He sat back and punched in another command. "Here. Look at this."

Miranda's arm came right in beside him, pointing to the computer screen. "That's what I saw. My brother saw it, too. For a couple of seconds, maybe."

"You saw this image?" The mainframe room, the brain center, of the GSS office building in the northern section of Kansas City stared back at them.

"Yes. There was a person there when I saw it. Could have been a man or woman, but it was just a glimpse. White coat. I couldn't see a face."

Quinn put on his glasses and picked up the phone on his desk. The late hour didn't matter. He paid his people good money to be roused at any time of day or night if there was an emergency. And this could be a big one.

He stared hard at the camera shot captured by the computer until a drowsy voice picked up. "Hello?"

"Ozzie? Quinn here. I need you to run a diagnostic on our computer system. I'll meet you at the lab first thing in the morning. I think somebody tapped into our mainframe."

"We've been hacked?" He could hear Ozzie Chang waking up. Sitting up. Going on alert. "Impossible."

"At the very least, somebody tried. I need you to get to the lab and run a full diagnostic on the system. Find out how deep it goes into our design work and programming. Bring in whatever help you need."

"I'm on it, boss."

After hanging up, Quinn took Miranda by the elbow and walked her to the door. "I'm going to be on the phone awhile longer. But you'd better get some sleep. It's already morning and I want you well rested for Fiona."

She planted her stockinged feet and turned in the doorway. "Is this something major?"

Quinn shrugged. "It's not the first time someone's tried to get into the GSS network. A good hacker could get his hands on some very sensitive, very costly information." Someone had gotten into GSS, but had they gotten beyond all the firewalls and passwords and layers of security code they'd built into the system? "I need to find out what programs, if any, were actually accessed."

"Do you think it's related to the threats?"

"There's no way to tell yet. It could be a diversion. Or, threatening my daughter could be the diversion that kept me occupied while someone tried to break in. It could be unrelated altogether." He touched the soft cotton of her sleeve again, dismissing her into the hallway. "There's no way to tell until my staff and I get in there and look."

"Mr. Gallagher—"

"Quinn. If we're going to be working together, living together, we might as well be on a first-name basis."

"Then I'm Randy."

"No, you're not." Quinn deliberately dropped his gaze to the tiny nips beading beneath her long-sleeve T-shirt, and the decadent flare of her backside in those soft flannel pants. And then he sought out the intriguing beauty of her eyes. There was nothing boyish about that strong body of hers, or his reaction to it. "Is it all right if I call you Miranda instead?"

"No one calls me…" Her lips parted on a heated breath and bowed out in a tempting curve the way they had earlier in the evening. He'd be kissing her before this week together was done, Quinn was certain of it. It might be a damn fool move, and he wished he had the strength to ignore the attraction arcing between them. When her tongue darted out to moisten the curve, and an answering heat sparked inside him, he was doubly certain it was going to happen. "Miranda's good."

"Thank you for bringing the computer malfunction to my attention." He brushed his fingers over the back of her hand, intrigued by the contrast of velvety softness and sinewy strength. He gently caught her in his grip and squeezed. "Good night, Miranda."

Her fingers tangled with his and squeezed back. "Good night, Quinn. Don't worry about Fiona. Do your job. And I'll do mine. I'll stay with her tonight."

He couldn't wait any longer for the inevitable. Cautious of any sign that he'd read this draw between them all wrong, Quinn dipped his head and pressed his lips against hers. They were warm, soft, as lushly tempting to the taste and touch as they'd been to the eye.

Her mouth opened slightly, moved beneath his, and he adjusted his stance to claim what she offered. Miranda braced her fist against his chest and rose onto her toes, sealing the bond between them more fully.

He thanked her for caring about his daughter, encouraged her to care a little about him, too. He caught her bottom lip between his, pulled on it gently, dabbed his tongue along the sleek, warm curve of it. Quinn shifted on his feet, instinctively wanting to move closer. He angled his mouth one way. She turned her mouth to fit his. Her tongue brushed his lips, darted to meet the tip of his. Her throat hummed with a breathy moan when he took command of the kiss again.

Their hands touched, their lips touched, and little more. It was just a kiss. A simple, tender, leisurely, getting-acquainted kind of kiss.

Yet Quinn sensed the low-burning flame kindling deep inside him, stirring in his blood. This kiss crossed the barriers of boss and employee, father and protector, professional and personal—clarifying them into basic man and basic woman, linking him to Miranda in ways that were too new and delicate and unexpected for him to process right now.

And he needed to be able to process. He needed to be in control of his thoughts and actions right now, especially when he wanted nothing more than to loosen that golden ponytail and tunnel his fingers into the silky cascade of Miranda's hair. He wanted to drive her back against that door frame and deepen the kiss, to feel that taut, slender body pressed against his. He wanted to fill his hands with that beautiful bottom and drag her up against the undeniable interest of his body.

Instead, Quinn ended the kiss, resting his forehead against hers. For a moment, he savored the gentle caresses of each stuttering breath against his cheek and lost himself in the drowsy passion in her eyes. "Wh-why did you kiss me?" she whispered.

Still looking to question him? Quinn smiled down at her. "Why did you kiss me back?"

Then he retreated a step, released her hand, let the cool night air of the house move between them. This wasn't the time for investigating just how far this attraction between them would go. It wasn't the time for giving in to wants. He had to leave if she wouldn't.

"We each have a job to do." He nudged her into the hallway and closed the door on temptation. "Good night."

Chapter Seven

4 Days until Midnight, New Year's Eve

Miranda sat across the breakfast table watching Fiona sticking the fruit-ring cereal she wasn't eating onto her fingers and onto her doll's nonexistent fingers, subsequently dropping most of them into her lap or onto the floor.

Miranda's own oatmeal and sliced bananas were eaten, the bowl and spoon washed. The second mug of coffee she'd poured herself had cooled. She wondered how many more bites of cereal could possibly be in that bowl, and just how long she was supposed to wait for the easily entertained little girl to either become full or tire of her creative jewelry making.

And while she sat and waited, Miranda noted how easily Fiona Gallagher smiled and laughed. Although the rich color of blue in her eyes was the same, their expression bore a marked contrast to her father.

Quinn Gallagher was more like Jekyll and Hyde than the comic-book alter egos he resembled physically. He was bossy and arrogant, used to people not questioning his orders. He was clever and stubborn and demanding. Yet he was heartsick and unsure about his daughter's safety. He was a vigilant protector of his home and family. He commanded a small staff and hundreds of employees and half the world's law enforcement and military supply lines, if the press about GSS was to be believed. Yet he seemed isolated and alone high in his ultramodern office and behind the tall, thick walls surrounding his home.

She was alone because her brother was overseas and she had no other family. She hadn't been able to develop really close relationships with the men she worked with because she was the newest member of the team, she was a woman, and she was the only member who wasn't at least married and starting a family. And she was so busy with work or training for work or worrying about work that she hadn't had much luck developing female friendships beyond the tentative bond she shared with Sergeant Delgado's wife, Josie. But Josie had a new baby, a new marriage and a new job as a trauma nurse. Miranda wasn't about to impose herself on Josie's time and put a strain on that one woman-to-woman bond. She'd become a pro at avoiding those fragile relationships that she seemed to have a talent for messing up in any number of ways.

Quinn Gallagher was alone because he'd lost the woman he'd loved to violence, and he wasn't about to care about anyone so deeply that it was worth the risk of losing someone else. He was alone because, like Miranda, he didn't quite fit in with the people around him. They deferred to him. They served him. They might even fear him. He was up on such a pedestal of wealth and power that people avoided getting too personal with him.

And yet, last night, in the silent shadows of a doorway warmed only by the lights of the Christmas tree in his study, two lonely people from two different worlds had connected. She and Quinn had created their own little world filled with hushed words and secret vows and a kiss.

A purple cereal ring bounced across the table and Miranda absently popped the sugary bite into her mouth, touching her lips and remembering that kiss.

In some ways, she supposed, it had been just a casual kiss. Other than her hand on the soft flannel of his robe and their lips, their bodies hadn't touched. Yet she'd been tempted to splay her fingers against the wall of his chest, to slide her palm inside to find the warmth of the skin she could feel through the velvety cotton.

No one had groped anything. Although even now, she could remember the pulsing grip of his hand around hers, as though his fingers were anxious to explore but unsure if they'd be welcome on her body.

His tongue had lightly tasted the tip of hers. His supple mouth had squeezed and pressed and gently suckled. The grip of Quinn's hand had been sure around hers—a support, a comfort, a connection.

Miranda couldn't remember ever being kissed like that—so gently, so thoroughly, so perfectly. Even now, in the wintry morning sunlight shining through the bank of windows in a cereal-studded kitchen, she could feel that kiss.

She'd gone all melty and gooey inside in a way that was totally at odds with the man and her mission. She'd sensed a power in Quinn, a potent male need held in check by the sheer strength of his will. And if that will had surrendered for even one moment, she suspected the warmth inside her would have exploded in a wild conflagration.

Remembering that kiss this morning made her temperature rise and her chest ache and parts of her body that had rarely been a priority ache to touch and be touched, to hold and be held, to kiss and be kissed again.

Quinn strode into the kitchen, startling Miranda from her thoughts. "I'm going into the office to meet with my chief software designer to make sure the computer simulation for that patent..." The remembered heat flooded her cheeks and she hid her face behind a sip of tepid coffee. Quinn pulled his leather gloves back off and tossed them onto the breakfast bar. "What is she doing?"

"Eating breakfast."

"She's making a mess."

Miranda rose to defend herself at the subtle accusation she heard in his voice. "Yes, but I figured I would wait until she was done and then clean everything up just one time."

Definitely Jekyll and Hyde. And there was no sign of the needy, passionate loner she'd connected with last night in the kitchen with her this morning. This was the GSS mogul, the brilliant eccentric, the man who gave orders—not the frightened father and tender lover who'd reached out to her in the shadows of the night.

He was dressed in a black wool coat, a suit and tie. Still, he reached for Fiona, lifted her from her booster seat and sat her in a clean chair at the side of the table to brush the bits and crumbs off her pajamas. "She was probably done twenty minutes ago. Get a washrag out of the drawer next to the sink and wet it."

Fiona held up her long, tiny fingers while Miranda found a cloth to clean her. "See my wings, Daddy?"

"I see them, sweetie." He nibbled one of the cereal rings off her finger and she chortled with delight. Quinn ate another bite from her hand, and another. By the time he'd polished them all off, she was belly-laughing and hugging him around the neck. He was a handsome man when he smiled and, frankly, a little intimidating when he didn't. Miranda wasn't feeling the love when he took the damp cloth from her fingers and started cleaning Fiona's face and fingers. "You really don't know anything about raising children, do you?" he said over the little girl's head.

Miranda bristled at the unfair attack. She'd been up front with him about her skill set when she'd agreed to this job. "I'm not on loan from KCPD because I have a way with kids."

He did not just roll his eyes, did he? "Are you at least armed?"

She tapped the back of her jeans and the weapon secured there. "24/7 this week. I'm keeping track of my Glock at all times since she's going to be around it."

"Good."

"Petwa?" Fiona reached for her doll in the messy chair.

In a surprising maneuver of multitasking efficiency, Quinn dabbed at the doll's face, then handed the doll to Fiona before giving Miranda the rag and some advice. "Fiona's a little girl. She doesn't eat all that much at a sitting. Try smaller portions and snacks throughout the day rather than three big meals. When she starts playing with her food, that's usually a sign that she's done."

"Thanks." So maybe a little bit of Dr. Jekyll had shown up this morning, after all. "I'll remember that."

"She can be taught."

Was that a joke? Even if it was at her expense, it was worth a smile. "Don't worry about the mess," she promised. "I'll clean up."

"Make sure you dress her warmly today. I'd like her to get some fresh air."

A brief moment of panic set in the moment he turned away. "What kind of games does she play outside?"

Quinn's eyes narrowed in that quizzical expression. "There's a foot of snow on the ground. What would *you* play?"

"Okay. I can do that." She breathed a little easier. Building snowmen and forts wouldn't be nearly as hard as figuring out the nighttime routine had been.

Cereal crunched beneath Quinn's shoe as he went back to the counter for his gloves and pulled his keys from his pocket. "Make sure you grab a radio from the command center and let them know when you go out and come back in. You've got a key card and understand the security codes?"

"Yes, sir." She patted the rear pocket of her jeans.

She wondered if Quinn's gaze had lingered an extra moment on the spot where she'd patted her hand. He adjusted the corner of his glasses, masking the exact angle of his eyes. "I should be home early this afternoon unless there's an issue with the simulation. And there won't be. I have to prove it works by noon."

That was a sobering reminder of the real reason she was here. "What happens if you can't do everything this guy asks?"

Quinn looked down at Fiona, who'd kicked off a slipper and was now picking up cereal with her toes. He bent over to kiss the crown of his daughter's hair. "I'm not giving him the chance to find out."

MIRANDA WAS FEELING LIKE a little girl herself as she ducked down behind the wall of the snow fort she and Fiona had built. It was an easy game of hide-and-seek, where they hid in the same place every time, and finding each other was all about the squeals of laughter and loud *Aha!*s of discovering a new friend.

Fiona's laughter was like a tonic to Miranda's doubting soul. In that little girl's eyes, the lopsided snowman and leaning fort wall were works of art. Conversations were simple and didn't always include words the other one understood, but there was real communication taking place. And despite the ever-present Petra and girly garb of pink on pink, from the topknot of her stocking cap to the toes of her tiny insulated boots, there were definite signs of a fellow tomboy lurking inside Fiona Gallagher.

Miranda held her breath as she heard the pink boots crunching in the snow and the breathy exertion of her companion scrambling over the top of the wall. She hunkered down in the icy snow, knowing there was no place for Fiona to land but on top of her.

"Aha! Found you."

Miranda rolled over, catching Fiona in her lap and laughing with her. "You found me. Yay!"

Obeying an unexpected impulse, Miranda hugged Fiona tight and kissed her cold, rosy cheek. When Fiona yanked her doll up between them, Miranda gladly kissed Petra's damp face, too.

It was so easy to fall in love with Fiona's sweet laugh and beautiful spirit, and Miranda was well on her way there. Her time outside with Quinn's daughter this morning was the best celebration of the winter holidays Miranda had enjoyed in a long time. She was relaxed, having fun, in delightful company.

But she wasn't about to forget her responsibilities. She pulled back the cuff of her coat to check the time. They'd been outside for almost an hour now. And though she'd bundled up Fiona in enough layers to resemble a small blimp in her snowsuit, she wasn't going to risk the chance of her getting chilled. Besides, Miranda's own stomach was beginning to grumble for a bite of lunch.

Using a newly acquired skill to encourage Fiona's cooperation, Miranda peeled off her glove to check the doll's muslin cheeks. "I think Petra's getting cold. Should we get her inside for some hot soup?"

Fiona mimicked the same touch with her pink mittens on the doll's face and agreed. "Petwa's cold."

"Okay. Let's go in." Miranda put her glove back on and dusted the snow from her jeans as she stood. Then she dusted the snow off Fiona's suit while Fiona brushed the snow off her doll.

A flash of light in the corner of her eye stopped Miranda from taking Fiona's hand. She turned her head, wondering what she'd seen. Scanning the wide expanse of the Gallagher acreage, though, she saw nothing but the creek, the tall white wall covered in ivy, the tops of the trees beyond and lots of undisturbed snow between them and the front gate. "Hmm."

Must have been the sun glinting off the snow, or the reflection from a windshield of a car along the street on the other side of the wall. She waited several seconds, spotting nothing unusual. And when she felt the grasp of Fiona's hand tugging at her fingers, she turned toward the house and headed for the mud room entrance off the kitchen.

Until she saw it again. Reflected in the glass of the outer storm door. Another flash of light.

Miranda spun around, pinpointing some kind of movement in the distance. She picked Fiona up in her arms and jutted out her right hip to carry her toward the house while she pulled the walkie-talkie David Damiani's men had assigned to her out of her pocket.

She was moving quickly across the snow toward the cleared sidewalk. She was hanging on to Fiona with one arm now, and the little girl was struggling to climb down. Miranda hitched her up against her side again and pressed the call button. "Holmes? You there? This is Officer Murdock."

The man stationed at the monitors in the command center this morning answered. "I'm here, Murdock. What's up?"

The radio communication amongst Damiani's crew wasn't as precise and polished as what Captain Cutler had drilled into her, but it was functional enough to serve its purpose. "I just saw a light, or reflection of one, on top of the north wall, west of the gate. I swear it looked like a camera flash. Or someone sending signals with a mirror." Fiona was squirming again. "I need you to sit tight, sweetie." The words meant nothing to the three-year-old and she squiggled free. "Fiona."

Where was she going?

Fiona waddled back to the fort and Miranda changed course to hurry after her.

"West of the gate, you said?" Holmes asked. Although she'd met the dark-haired man Christmas Day passed out in the car with another guard and the bloody doll, they really hadn't had a chance to get acquainted beyond basic introductions. Maybe the guy was hard of hearing.

"Yes. Approximately thirty yards. Can't tell if it's from the top of the wall or in one of the trees on the other side." Something up there was definitely moving. And then the light flashed again. Son of a gun. Some perp was spying on them. Oh, for a pair of binoculars right about now. "I just saw it again. You want me to investigate?"

"I'll have Rowley walk the perimeter and check it out."

"Tell him to get there fast. This guy's on the move. Murdock out." Fiona was back at the fort, climbing over the wall again. "Fiona. Come here!"

"Petwa find me."

"No." It was time for the game to stop. "You need to listen to me."

Fiona dived into the snow just as Miranda reached for her.

Just as a man stood up on top of the wall fifty yards away.

Miranda's internal alarm kicked into overdrive. She glanced down at Fiona, half-buried in the snow. She glanced up at the man who was bundled up enough from head to toe to make it impossible to get a read on his face at this distance. Ah, hell. Was he climbing down inside the property?

Giving one more look to assure herself that Fiona was hidden from sight behind the wall of the fort, Miranda followed the urgency to meet the threat head-on that sparked through every nerve ending. "You stay here with Petra, sweetie. You hide and I'll come find you."

The man was scrambling to cling to the top of the bricks now. He must have slipped in the snow on top and was desperately trying to find a toehold and pull himself back up. But what was he doing here in the first place?

Miranda reached beneath her coat and pulled her gun. She clasped it firmly between her hands, barrel pointed down as she ran through the snow to the driveway. She crossed the creek and stopped at the last pylon of the bridge over it, raising her gun with a steady aim and raising her voice. "KCPD! You're trespassing on private property! Put your hands up and identify yourself."

With a heave that was all muscle, the man swung a leg up on top of the wall and pulled himself over. But something he was wearing caught in the ivy vines and pulled him off balance. He swore, a low, muffled sound.

"KCPD!" she shouted again. She fished the walkie-talkie out of her pocket and hit the call button. "Holmes! He's getting away! Holmes! Rowley! Is anybody out front? Somebody talk to me."

Miranda sprang to her feet as he jerked free and dropped down on the opposite side of the wall. The thing around his neck—the camera, maybe?—hit the bricks and tumbled down through the ivy on the wall. The instinct to pursue jolted through her legs, but he was already out of sight. She pointed her gun up above the treetops and fired a warning shot. "KCPD! Stop!"

As soon as the loud pop of her gun rent the air, a high-pitched squeal sounded behind her. Miranda lowered her weapon and turned as Fiona, startled by the loud noise, burst into tears.

"Oh, sweetie." Miranda tucked her gun in the back of her jeans. "Oh, no." What had she done? She squatted down and reached for the girl. "Don't. Don't do that." She scooped her up in a tight hug and the girl wrapped her arms around Miranda's neck and bawled into her ear. "What are you doing here, sweetie? I thought you were hiding."

Now she was tired of playing the game?

She stood with Fiona in her arms, cradling her head against her neck and rocking her from side to side. "That was a gun, sweetie. See why you should never play with one? It's loud and scary and it could hurt you." Fiona squealed again and clung even tighter. Miranda didn't understand. "Do you think I'm hurt? I'm not hurt." Then she turned her face away from the girl and shouted her frustration. "Somebody talk to me!"

"Who fired that shot?" Holmes's voice buzzed over the walkie-talkie. "Do I need to lock it down?"

"What?" There was a loud thunk of metal on metal at the front gate, followed by smooth whirring noises, like the pulsing chirp of a million grasshoppers, from the entrance to the estate and the house behind her. "No!" They were engaging the reinforced steel gate while steel shutters were coming down over every door and window of the house. "Fiona will be stranded out here in the open. Stop what you're doing and go after that guy!"

Over a second thunk and the whirring noises of the steel barriers disengaging, Miranda heard the snapping of twigs, a thump and a curse in the distance. And then she heard the distinctive sound of a door slamming and a car speeding away.

"I missed him." Finally, Rowley reported in, after a punch of static from the walkie-talkie in her pocket. "The guy fell about halfway down the wall. He's hurt, but I couldn't catch him. The car came up out of no-where."

Miranda stepped into the snow on the far side of the creek and headed for the ivy wall as she pulled out the walkie-talkie. "Did you get a plate number?"

"A partial. He was already in the car by the time I reached him. He's long gone now." Fiona seemed to like the bumpy trip of being carried across the deep, undisturbed snow. Her cries had quieted to whimpers and sniffles, although her hold on Miranda's neck was as snug as ever. "It's not the same car you saw," Rowley added. "It's another black Beemer, but the first digits on the license I saw were different."

Miranda was blind to events from this side of the wall, and she wasn't sure she trusted the report. She would have given chase, shot out a tire, scaled that wall, if she didn't have Fiona with her. Just what kind of incompetents did Quinn have working for him here? They'd gotten drugged. They let a suspect escape. They'd nearly locked her and Fiona out of the house. At least he'd gotten the make of the car and a partial plate.

She was at the wall now. She paused for a moment to wipe away the tears freezing on Fiona's cheeks, and smiled. "Can I set you down now?"

Fiona shook her head and thrust herself against Mi-randa's chest.

Miranda hugged her, stroked her back...and got an idea.

"Do you want to help me?" she asked. She made it

sound like the adventure of a lifetime. "I need you to climb the wall."

Boom. Just like that, the whimpers stopped and Fiona leaned back.

"That's my girl." Miranda pointed to the camera hanging in the torn ivy, just above her reach. "Can you get that for me?"

With an enthusiastic nod, Fiona let Miranda turn her in her arms and lift her onto her shoulders. Then she leaned against the cushion of ivy and pushed Fiona up. "Can you reach it?"

Like the closet monkey she was, Fiona braced one hand against the wall and grabbed the camera. When she tugged it loose, it crashed into the snow and popped open.

In spite of her tear-chapped cheeks, Fiona was all smiles when Miranda set her down. "I climb," she said proudly.

Squatting down, Miranda hugged her to her side. "You sure did, sweetie. You did a good job."

Miranda dug the broken camera out of the snow. It was an older model, one that made instant snapshots. She pulled out the last photo that had gotten stuck in the mechanism and shook the snow off it. Moisture dotted and smeared the image, but the subject was clear—it was a picture of her and Fiona playing in the snow.

The guy must have been watching them for at least twenty minutes. And the guard at the gate hadn't noticed him?

"Murdock?" Holmes was calling her on the walkie-talkie again. "You there? Are you and Fiona safe?"

She pushed the button to answer. "We're safe. Go ahead and call Captain Cutler—and your chief, Damiani—to report the guy taking pictures. Ask if there's any follow-up we need to do."

"I've already got Damiani on the line. Say, Murdock?"

"Yes?"

"You know, you didn't have to panic like that."

Panic? Miranda steamed. That nincompoop of a snail was accusing her of panicking at the intruder?

"If you get locked out of the house, there's an override on the second-story windows. The boss designed it that way in case there was a fire, so no one would get trapped inside. The steel shutters up there are built on a flexible hinge. Just jimmy it with something small like a screwdriver, and the shutter will pop open."

"Jimmy it with a screwdriver. Got it." It might have been nice to let her know that before this place locked down like a prison. Weren't they all on the same team, trying to protect this family? "Murdock out."

She looped the camera strap over her shoulder and picked up Fiona, taking care to hold the picture so it didn't sustain any further damage and there was some chance the crime lab could analyze it. With each step back to the house, her pace slowed as her protective temper abated and those familiar doubts crept back into her head. Did she really have room to complain about the quality of Gallagher's security force?

She hadn't noticed the spy until he'd already taken several pictures, either.

"WORKS LIKE A DREAM, BOSS." Ozzie Chang hit the print command and rocked back in his chair in the GSS computer lab. "In theory, anyway." He pulled a pen from his spiky black hair and marked a couple of reference points on the printout. "Although, I still don't get why you wanted to run a simulation program on the old electronic locks. Are we really going to start building these again? This is like two models and a whole bunch of out-of-date source codes ago."

Quinn squeezed Ozzie's thin shoulder as he checked the time on the clock. 11:32. Just in time before the noon deadline. He needed to get someplace private and send the updated design to the anonymous email address. "Thanks, Oz. I'm just feeling sentimental," he lied. There was no need to involve anyone else in this game he'd been forced to play. "I wanted to see if there was any value in revitalizing the old program."

"Yeah, but over Christmas? I figured you were a workaholic, man, but even I took the day off to play a marathon of 'Zombie Apocalypse' with my buds online."

To each their own way of celebrating the holidays. Although he was anxious to be on his way and get the job completed by the deadline, Quinn grinned at the young man. "Did you win?"

"Kicked their butts into the New Age, sir."

Quinn breathed out a reluctant sigh and pushed his glasses onto the bridge of his nose. Had he ever been that young and carefree? Growing up had been about working to help his mom make ends meet. It was about learning to outrun the bullies, then learning to outwit them as he got older. A few times, it had been about a four-eyed kid learning how to fight—to defend himself, and to defend his mother from some of the desperate choices she had made.

It had rarely been about holiday celebrations and playing games where the biggest consequence was developing sore thumbs from too many hours at the game controller.

There was a lot to envy about Ozzie's young-at-heart attitude. He was glad to have that kind of young energy working at GSS. "Would you email the data to my office address?"

"Sure thing, boss." With a spin of his chair, Ozzie was typing at the keyboard again. "Email sent. Anything else?"

Quinn swiped his key card and punched in the code to leave the lab. But he paused at the open door. "Yeah. Go home. Call your folks. Call your friends. Do whatever it is you do that makes you happy. I don't want to see you again until after the New Year. And look for a bonus in next month's paycheck."

"Sweet."

"Can you lock up the shop?"

Ozzie grinned. "Yes, sir. Happy New Year."

"Happy New Year to you."

Quinn didn't wait for the door to close behind him. He jogged to the bank of elevators and got inside to press the penthouse office button.

As soon as he was in his office, he logged into the company server and pulled up the email from Ozzie. Then, with a grim sense of foreboding, he emailed the file to the anonymous email address he'd been given and waited.

He wasn't quite sure how updating the design specs on an old security system, and proving it still worked, would make things "right" for his tormentor. He had a feeling the task had been more about busywork, a diversion of some kind. But he wasn't going to argue the inanity of the task. He was simply going to do it and pray it would be enough to remove Fiona as a target in this anonymous bastard's scheme.

His phone vibrated in his chest pocket and he inhaled a deep, steadying breath before answering it. There were still four days to go until the New Year. He'd been threatened by too many bullies growing up to believe this was actually going to stop without some kind of major fight.

He read the text message on his phone screen.

Nicely done, Mr. G. Your daughter gets to live for another day. You will be hearing from me tomorrow. And trust me, the message will be loud and clear.

Chapter Eight

3 Days until Midnight, New Year's Eve

Louis Nolan paced the sitting area of Quinn's office. The receding points of his hairline wrinkled with the tension radiating off him. "Nervous investors are bad for business, especially when we're about to start a new fiscal year. We're talking millions of dollars here, Quinn. He's come all the way from Europe. The least you can do is hear him out."

"I'm a little busy right now, Louis." Quinn glanced up from the printout where he'd been reviewing the simulation data provided by Ozzie Chang. He'd been an idiot—a full-fledged, too-smart-for-his-own-good-so-he'd-overlooked-the-obvious idiot. The reason for the busywork and the noon deadline yesterday was hidden right here, in the thousands of lines of code that ran the program. He and Ozzie had provided the means for a talented hacker to get into the GSS network.

It was impossible to tell how successful the break-in had been from this printout. He'd already made certain that the thousands of home security systems they monitored hadn't been compromised, so this wasn't about a spree of pending burglaries. And it would be a long, painstaking process to go through all of GSS's data files and employees' personal computers to see if any of them had been tapped into, downloaded or stolen.

This was his own damn fault. He'd been so distracted by the Kalahari explosion and the trespasser taking pictures of his daughter and the sick threats against his family that he'd made an amateur mistake. The hacker had tapped into the GSS mainframe through the trapdoor created when he'd run that simulation program. Now he needed a way to backtrack to the source and eliminate any other inroads into GSS and its systems.

You will be hearing from me tomorrow. And trust me, the message will be loud and clear.

Tomorrow was now today, and Quinn didn't want any more surprises. If he could figure out the target inside the GSS mainframe, then maybe he could finally get ahead of this creep and stop him. "This is where my talents are best put to use today. I trust you to handle the situation with Titov."

His attention drifted to the tiny brunette playing at the far end of his office, and the tall blonde sitting dutifully still while Fiona listened to her heart with a plastic stethoscope and put bandages all over Miranda's dark blue sweater. He'd hired the best security in the city— heck, he'd invented and developed some of the best security technology in the world. And yet he couldn't shake the irrational fear that letting Fiona out of his sight meant not being able to protect her.

Finding out who'd dared to threaten his family, and stopping him, were the only things on Quinn's to-do list right now.

Louis slapped his palm on Quinn's desk the moment he returned his attention to the printout. "That's what I'm trying to tell you. I don't know that I *can* handle it. I've reassured him every way I know how, but Nikolai insists on talking directly to you."

"You're the one who has the rapport with him. You're the one who brokered the deal to keep his money in GSS after we closed the plant in Lukinburg." No matter how influential an investor was, or how much clout he carried in the European market, nothing was more important than his daughter's safety. Until Quinn could determine whether or not the attack on the GSS security network was part of that threat, or another distraction that was diverting his attention from his daughter, his focus needed to be right here. He summoned up a reassurance for his COO. "You're my right hand in this company, Louis. I know you can handle Nikolai Titov."

"As your right hand, you've always trusted me to take care of the business side of things—no matter what else is going on with your life. I kept things running for months while you dealt with Valeska's murder. I've helped you weather wars and economic crashes. I know you're worried about Fiona right now." Louis's bushy silver brows lifted with a friendly beseechment. "But this company is her future, too. A short meeting to alleviate the concerns of one of our most important partners is all I'm asking from you right now. Ten minutes of your time this morning, and I'll be able to keep the European market afloat for us while you see to the needs of your family."

It was Louis's job to put the company first. As much as the timing stank, Quinn was a smart enough man to listen to the experts he'd hired.

"You know, Louis, anyone else talking to me like this would be downright irritating. But I know you're thinking of the bigger picture when I can't. All right. Ten minutes." He slipped the printout into the top right drawer of his desk and called his assistant. "Elise? Show Mr. Titov and his associates into my office."

"Yes, Quinn. Right away."

Pushing back his chair as he stood, Quinn rolled down his sleeves and buttoned his cuffs. He circled around his desk to grab his suit jacket off the back of one of the sofas and kept on walking until he reached Miranda and Fiona. He buttoned his collar and tightened his tie before squatting down to Fiona's level. "Hey, sweetie. Daddy has to do a little work now. Why don't you and Miranda go check out the break room and get a snack? Do you remember the way?"

Fiona grinned from ear to ear. "Soda pop."

"That's right. It's where the soda pop machine is." Quinn shook his head and directed his wishes to Miranda, who was on her knees peeling off bandages. "Make sure she drinks juice. Go to the elevator and follow the hallway around."

"I saw the room during our search on Christmas Eve." Miranda stood, her expression concerned behind Fiona's back. "Trouble?"

Quinn hugged his daughter and set her on her feet before standing. "Business."

When he took Fiona's hand and pressed it into Miranda's, his fingers brushed against hers. His sensitive fingertips tingled at the brief contact, remembering where a simple holding of hands had led them the night before last. Just as quickly, he pulled away before he could get sucked into a distraction like that again. He needed a clear head to deal with Titov and Louis's concerns so he could be done with them and get back to his investigation into the hacked computer system.

Still, when a woman had a green mermaid bandage stuck to her shoulder, it was a gentleman's duty to remove it for her. He peeled the strip of plastic off Miranda's sweater. The movement brought him close enough to look over her shoulder to see the bulge of her gun at the back of her waist. Right. Tingling skin and remembered kisses had no place between them. As much as he hated the idea of a gun being so close to his daughter, the idea of a three-year-old being completely defenseless against an unseen threat frightened him even more. "Don't let her out of your sight."

"I won't."

"Right this way, gentlemen." The office door opened before Miranda and Fiona reached it. Elise Brown, who'd interrupted her visit with her parents to come in this morning, made Quinn think this was any other day at the GSS offices—for a moment. The last few days had left his brain in perpetual turmoil—solving riddles, being stymied by Miranda's sexy quirks and, unpredictability, protecting his daughter. Elise's stylish suit, cordial smile and efficient manner added a touch of normalcy to the room that Quinn needed in order to deal with a man like Titov. Nikolai and two of his associates came in, and Elise gestured to the seating area in the middle of the office suite. "Make yourselves comfortable wherever you like."

Quinn was shaking hands and being introduced to Nikolai's accountant and a Lukinburger stock analyst when a dark-haired dynamo dashed back into the room.

"Petwa!" Fiona darted through the middle of the gathering to retrieve her doll from the box of toys where they'd been playing.

"Sorry, sir," Miranda apologized from the doorway. "We forgot her sidekick."

"She doesn't go anywhere without Petra. Her mother made it for her when she was born." Quinn passed his hand over the silky crown of Fiona's dark waves as she zigzagged back through the towers of amused adults in her path.

Before she reached Miranda, Nikolai Titov picked Fiona up in his arms. Quinn was more startled than his daughter seemed to be, but Louis's calming hand on his arm stopped him from taking more than half a step toward them. Miranda was moving right up behind Titov. Quinn still had her in his sight. Despite the emotional jolt that quickened his heart rate, logically he knew his daughter was safe.

"What a beauty you are." Nikolai offered Fiona a fatherly sort of smile as he tucked a curl behind the little girl's ear. His accented voice trilled the *r*'s and punctuated each consonant. "She looks so like your Valeska, does she not, Quinn?"

Quinn met the sincere appreciation in Nikolai's gaze and nodded. Had it been that long since he and Nikolai had met face-to-face? That last dinner together on the Plaza, when Val had been pregnant with Fiona? No wonder Louis was worried about Titov and his foreign investors losing faith in GSS.

"Fortunately, Fiona takes after the better-looking parent."

Fiona poked at Nikolai's silver-and-black goatee. "Are you a gwandpa?"

"No. Unfortunately, I never will be. I have no children." He gave her a noisy kiss on the cheek.

Everyone in the room laughed except for Miranda, who lifted Fiona from Nikolai's arms and caught her by the hand. "She gets her smarts and curiosity from her father." Her warm smile included each of the guests in the room. "You all have business to discuss, so we'll, um, go do some exploring."

Quinn wondered at the lack of a smile when her eyes reached him. The double shifting of her gaze toward the door sent a clearer message, however. "Excuse me a moment, gentlemen. Elise? If you'd be so good as to pour our guests some coffee?"

"Of course. Mr. Titov…" Elise took over the meeting for a moment as Quinn slipped away to meet Miranda at the door.

"What is it?" he asked in a whisper.

Miranda pulled her ponytail from the front of her shoulder and flicked it down the middle of her back.

She answered in an equally hushed yet urgent voice. "Mr. Titov's *accountant* is wearing a gun in an ankle holster."

An armed man in his office? Quinn stiffened his neck against the impulse to turn and confirm her observation. But the more rational side of his brain wouldn't let him panic. "He wouldn't be the first wealthy man to hire a bodyguard."

Her eyes blanched wide as she remembered her own position, then narrowed. "Once we're out of here, I'm calling Mr. Damiani down in the security office to make sure he checked these guys out thoroughly."

"Get her out of here." Quinn hurried them out the door and readied to close it behind them. "Don't stray too far," he called after them for the benefit of the others in the room.

He appreciated her firm grip on Fiona. "We won't."

Quinn adjusted his glasses at the temple, giving himself a moment to blank the suspicion from his face before returning to his guests. Putting out fires with a primary investor was not how he wanted to be spending the day. But Nikolai Titov was worth millions to GSS. And he'd only be separated from Fiona for the ten minutes it took to reassure him of his importance to the company.

"Nikolai, please." He strolled back to the center of the room, positioning himself to verify the gun on the beefy accountant's leg, and to see if he could spot whether anyone else was armed. "You've been on a flight for twenty hours. Sit and relax. We have plenty of time to talk." He smiled as Elise carried a tray of coffee cups and a pot to the long table between the sofas. "You remember my executive assistant, Elise, don't you?"

"Yes." Nikolai actually took the tray and set it down for her. "You are looking as beautiful as ever, is she not, Quinn?"

Huh? Oh, yeah. Elise was a pretty woman. Talented. Skilled. Loyal. But she was, well, Elise. He'd never thought of her as anything but the boon she was to the company. She'd worked for him for ten years now. Elise he understood. Quinn's gaze slid over to the door Miranda had just exited. Understanding that one, on the other hand...?

"Thank you, Mr. Titov." Elise was blushing under the continental charm of their guest. "Well, if you need anything else..."

Nikolai frowned as she handed him the china cup and saucer. "You are not joining us for the meeting, Miss Brown?"

"Quinn?"

What the hell? Was Nikolai thinking of stealing his top assistant? Or did he just have a thing for brunettes? He had no reason to question Elise's loyalty. And since she was privy to pretty much everything at the company, anyway... "That's fine with me." Perhaps Louis was right, and he needed to give their guests his full attention in order to stave off a different sort of threat to everything he'd built. Quinn refused a cup of coffee for himself and gestured to the sofas and chairs. "Please. Have a seat."

"How was your holiday?" Elise asked, joining Nikolai on the sofa across from the men who'd accompanied him from Lukinburg.

Nikolai sipped his coffee and sighed. "I cannot celebrate at a time like this."

"What's wrong, Mr. Titov?" she asked.

"Nikolai, please."

Quinn went to the window and looked out at the snowy white landscape, and the airport control tower and hotels on the horizon. "You should have called before flying all the way to the States, Nikolai."

"This cannot wait. I do not like what I am hearing, half a world away."

"What are you hearing in St. Feodor?" Louis asked.

Quinn heard the rattle of a cup and saucer behind him, and saw Nikolai's reflection in the window as he approached. "I heard about the Kalahari plant being destroyed. Is it the work of terrorists?"

"No way to know yet. No factions I know of have taken credit for it."

"I gave you a million dollars for that and pledged ten more. We were going to make military-grade drones. And now we have nothing."

"My insurance will cover your lost investment, Nikolai."

"But what about the future profit I have lost? Who will pay the millions you promised me?"

Quinn slipped his hands into the pockets of his slacks and faced the shorter man. "Other than the tragic loss of life in the explosion and fire, this is something GSS will recover from."

"But when?" Nikolai pointed a stubby finger at

Quinn's chin. "If you do not get that plant up and running soon, my investors in Lukinburg will be very disappointed." He dropped his voice to a whisper. "And these are not the type of men you want to disappoint."

Did that explain the armed accountant? Had Nikolai received some sort of threat, as well?

Quinn shook his head and turned away, flattening his palm against the cool glass, struggling to maintain an equally cool, unemotional facade when everything inside him was arguing to end this discussion and get back to the work of tracking down the enemy who wanted to destroy him.

"It's not like I can get the plant up and running again in a matter of days. Or even weeks." The glimmer of an idea popped into his head. Days. Time line. *Make it right.* Had he offended somebody? Shortchanged anyone by green-lighting the Kalahari project? *Do I have your attention now?* Why wouldn't destroying the plant be enough? Why come after his daughter? Why not just ask for more money?

Maybe it was just the countdown to New Year's weighing on his mind and getting mixed up with Nikolai's visit that made him think he was onto finding an answer here.

A little of that frustration crept into Quinn's voice. "Whoever planted those bombs razed it to the ground. We're talking about months of rebuilding."

"My partners in Lukinburg were expecting to see results in a few months." The strain of remaining civil raised the volume in Nikolai's voice. "Now we are talking about delaying profits for a year or more."

"You knew the risks."

Louis joined them at the window and tried to play peacemaker. "Nikolai, your investors aren't the only ones who lost money. Some of us here at GSS put our own funds into that project. We took a hit, too."

"Then I have a solution for you, Mr. Nolan." But Nikolai's answer was aimed squarely at Quinn. "The GSS plant in St. Feodor that you closed last year. Move the drone-assembly operation there. The building and assembly lines are still in place. We have the rail lines and a small airport nearby. It could work."

"We closed the St. Feodor plant because it was too small. And the cost for refitting it for a new product—"

"—would be offset because you would not have to rebuild the entire facility. And you know we have the skilled workers there." Nikolai must have been planning this speech all the way from Lukinburg. "Many are still out of work since the plant closed. I think I could convince my investors to put up the money again if they know they are investing in the benefit of their homeland."

Ten minutes and making nice was done. "I'll consider it, Nikolai. But just now I have another issue that is quite urgent I must attend to. Let me call you after the New Year. Perhaps Louis could take a trip to Lukinburg to look over the condition of the plant and discuss it further." He nodded toward Elise, who could read him well enough to know when he wanted to end a meeting and began ushering their guests toward the door. "He could take my assistant with him."

Elise and Nikolai made some eye contact at the door.

To Quinn's surprise, but apparently to Elise's pleasure, Nikolai raised her knuckles to his lips and kissed her hand. "That would be most agreeable."

"I'd look forward to it," Elise agreed.

Nikolai released her to hold a hand out to Quinn. "Do not wait too long, my friend. The investors I speak of are not patient men."

The questionable nature of some of Titov's investors had been another reason to close the St. Feodor plant. But Quinn didn't have the time, nor was he in the right frame of mind, to bring up that topic or make any major business decisions right now.

He was reaching out to shake Nikolai's hand when the elevator doors opened on the far side of Elise's office and David Damiani came charging out. "Quinn? Quinn!"

"What the...?"

David was a linebacker, running straight at the quarterback. "I couldn't risk calling your cell. We need to evacuate the building."

"What's wrong?"

Going on instant alert, Quinn wondered if Miranda would hear the shouting or feel the tension multiplying on the top floor. Was she drawing her gun? Getting Fiona as far away from the security chief's alarm as she could?

"Everyone needs to turn off their cell phones. Landlines only if you need to make a call." The big man pushed past their guests, and ran to Quinn's desk. "Have you checked your emails? We need to get these people out of here."

"David. Answers. Now."

"We've been monitoring all computer activity since that...glitch yesterday." David flipped on the computer and pulled Quinn behind the desk, urging him to type in his password and pull up his files. "Phones off?" he prompted to the others in the room.

One by one, everyone but Elise pulled out cell phones and complied. "Mine's in my purse at my desk," she said.

"Get it," David ordered.

"Quinn?" Miranda shouted from the hallway.

David saw her at the elevator now, too. "Elise, tell the nanny to turn off her phone."

"Ah, hell." Quinn looked through the glass walls of his office. No, no, no, no, no. Miranda was running toward them. She had her phone in one hand and Fiona in the other. "David, talk to me."

"Here." David highlighted an email and opened it. He turned the monitor to Quinn and pointed to the screen. "Ozzie Chang found this encrypted in the system. I verified it myself and evacuated the lab."

Quinn frowned. "What's Ozzie doing here? I told him to take a vacation."

"Does it matter?" David tapped the monitor. "Look."

"Son of a bitch."

Another day of this nightmare. Another threat.

As promised, the message was a hauntingly clear photo of the GSS computer lab. And the open briefcase with the wires and timer and C-4 sitting on the table in the middle of the lab had nothing to do with computers at all. The picture was framed by a rotating word stream that read, *See? I can get to everything that belongs to you. Make it right. Tick. Tock. Tick. Tock...*

"Make it...?" The blood in Quinn's brain drained to his toes before adrenaline pumped his heart into overtime. "What the hell do you want from me?" He swung around to the others. "There's a bomb in the building. Everybody out of here! Now!"

"That's the same picture I saw when I was talking to my brother."

"Damn it, Miranda." She was right beside him, looking at the same picture, reading the same threat. "Your job is to protect my daughter. Get out of here."

"I sent her with Elise. She'll be safe. That's enough plastique to take out a couple of floors." She picked up the corded telephone on Quinn's desk. "Damiani, take those people down the stairs. We can't risk anyone getting stuck in the elevator. Is there anyone else in the building?"

"Sir?" David was questioning who was in charge here.

Quinn plucked the phone from Miranda's fingers and handed it to David as he pushed her toward the door. "You stay with my daughter."

With a twist of her body, she freed her arm from Quinn's grasp and hurried back to the desk. "Get real, Quinn. This is exactly the type of situation I'm trained for. *You* need to get out of here with Fiona and let me work." She turned to David. "Is everyone out of the building?" she repeated.

The big man nodded. "Every person who signed in at the front desk has been accounted for now. There's hardly anyone here over the holidays, but I've got my men doing a floor-by-floor search, just in case."

"Have you called the police?"

"Already spoke to your friend Cutler. His team is on the way. Local cops are clearing a perimeter around the nearby businesses."

She picked up the phone again and punched in a number. "Where is the lab located?" she asked.

"Fourth floor," David answered.

Her call picked up. "Yes, sir, this is Murdock. I'm at GSS headquarters now." Michael Cutler must be on the line. She was all business, all focus now, as she pointed to the computer screen. "Can we print this out?"

David hit the print command while *Officer* Murdock answered another question. "Nine souls on the top floor." She stretched over the desk to see through the glass wall. "Four men, a woman and a child are coming down the northeast stairwell."

Quinn remained a step behind her, unheeded, fuming. "What about Fiona?"

"You don't think I can do more good for her dealing with the bomb than holding her hand?"

"What if that bomb's a dummy and this is all a ruse to get Fiona outside, unprotected?"

She glanced up at David. He muttered a curse and shook his head, understanding the silent request. "My job is to protect this man and this company."

As much as Quinn wanted Miranda out of here with Fiona, he knew what needed to be done. He motioned David to the door. "Your job is to do what I say. She's right."

"I don't like leaving you up here."

"We'll be right behind you in a few minutes. I won't have any other deaths on my conscience. My daughter is your top priority. Get her someplace safe. Go."

"Don't let Dirty Harriet here screw up our protocols. If I don't see you outside in fifteen minutes, I'm coming back in."

As far as Quinn could tell, security was already screwed up if someone had gotten inside GSS to place a bomb. The idea that anyone could get past all the systems he'd invented and put to use smacked of an inside job. But with the clock ticking and people in danger, he didn't have the luxury of speculation right now. With a nod from his boss, the security chief, David, hustled out the door as quickly as he'd barged in.

Quinn pulled the photo from the printer and tried to make out the bomb's schematics while Miranda glared at him across the desk. "You should go, too."

"You stay," he challenged, "I stay."

All at once her posture changed. She was talking on the phone again. "No. I can't, sir." She squeezed her eyes shut and mouthed a curse. "My gear's in my truck, back at the estate. I rode in with Quinn and Fiona. All I have on me is my sidearm."

"Miranda?"

"But—" Whatever Michael Cutler was saying transformed the bullheaded cop into a woman far less sure of herself. "Understood, sir. Yes, I will. Murdock out."

She hung up the phone. "Captain Cutler will be here in ten minutes to take charge of the scene. He wants the building clear by that time, too. In the meantime, I don't suppose you have an extra flak vest lying around?"

"Come with me." Quinn reached across the desk and grabbed her hand, pulling her into a jog out the door with him. Finally, something he had an answer for. "GSS makes them." A few seconds later, he unlocked a storage closet beside the break room and shoved aside a box marked Gas Masks and one labeled Flash Bangs before opening a third crate and pulling out two vests. "We keep samples of these and other nonlethal products in the building. We use them as visual aids in our sales presentations."

"I can only wear one."

"I'm coming with you." He pulled off his jacket and tie and strapped on the vest. "I'm guessing Michael told you to get the hell out of the building, and you plan to go take a look at that bomb, anyway, before you leave."

At least she didn't bother denying her intent. She secured the Velcro straps beneath each arm, then checked her gun to make sure she could still easily access it with the vest on. "I need to get eyes on that device so I can describe it to the bomb squad when they arrive. Why are you still here?"

She ran to the stairwell and Quinn chased after her. "I'm the bomb squad."

"What?" She stopped in her tracks on the stairwell's concrete landing, and Quinn plowed into her back. He got a brief imprint of sleek curves and heat against his harder thighs before he grabbed her arms and pulled her back from the steel railing. She turned to face him. "You think you're going to defuse that bomb?"

"I build bomb components in one of my GSS divisions. I've designed half the electronics in that picture myself. Chances are I can defuse it before any of KCPD's experts can get here."

Miranda's hand came to the middle of his chest and pushed him back to arm's length. "We are not leaving this to chance."

He leaned forward, pressing into her hand. "I'm not arguing with you on this."

"Rule 2 of my job is to get eyes on the threat. As officer on the scene, that's *my* responsibility." She slid her hand up the vest and cupped his cheek. "Rule 1 is to protect civilians and prevent casualties. You need to be outside, out of harm's way."

Quinn reached up to cover her hand with his, wondering if she was aware of just how much concern was shining from her eyes, and just how afraid he was for her and Fiona, in return. "*My* building. *My* people. I'm the captain of this ship. You don't think I can do more good for my daughter dealing with the bomb than holding her hand?" Her eyes widened when he threw her own words back at her. He leaned in, stopping up her protest with a quick kiss to ease the sting and trade a bit of reassurance. Now to toss some infallible logic into a debate he refused to lose. "Do you know where the lab is located?"

"Fourth floor. I can find it on my own. You need to leave."

"Do you know the code to get inside?"

With a sigh of resignation and a squeeze of his hand, she pulled away. "Fine. Lead the way, Captain."

Chapter Nine

Miranda clipped the spare radio Sergeant Rafe Delgado had brought her from the SWAT van to her collar, and adjusted the earpiece before testing it. "Captain Cutler, this is Murdock. Can you hear me?"

Michael Cutler's voice buzzed over the connection. "Loud and clear, Murdock. Now give me eyes on what you're seeing."

She went back into the sterile white computer lab to find both Quinn and the sergeant examining the brief-case bomb with flashlights and an assortment of tools. A lump of worry caught in her throat to see the con-trasts between the two men. Rafe, the team's explosives expert, was suited up from head to toe in protective armor. But Quinn had only whatever protection the flak vest and his tailored wool trousers could provide. He wasn't wearing a helmet. Heck, he wasn't even wearing his glasses. Instead, they lay on the tabletop beside the case while he leaned over, his face mere inches from the bomb itself.

But none of that was what the captain wanted to hear. She swallowed the lump and relied on her training to get her through this. "Sarge and Mr. Gallagher think they can disarm it. They're removing the firing pins from the C-4 blocks." She moved in close enough to look over Quinn's shoulder. "I think the trick is going to be removing the firing mechanisms from the briefcase itself. It's tangled up pretty good in there, with several redundant systems. They're going through them one by one, but the timer's down to—" she read the thin red numbers counting down on the digital clock in a beat more steady than her own heart "—seventeen minutes. Even an accidental connection with the electrical current might set off a chain reaction that could still blow everything."

"Are we all clear on the time?" the captain asked, including the rest of the team. "Everyone is out of the building in fifteen minutes. No exceptions."

"Captain?" Rafe tapped his mike and added to the report. "I can safely remove about half of the C-4 without disturbing anything. But if Gallagher can't turn this off, there'll still be enough explosive left to take out this room. I recommend bringing in the box."

"Roger that." The "box" was a heavily reinforced metal container with specially designed baffles inside. It was used to detonate a theoretically controlled explosion so that no shrapnel would be thrown out to cause injury or damage. Still, an explosion was an explosion, a wild mess of forced air and flying debris, a potentially deadly risk to everyone in the area. The captain called another member of the team. "Trip, what's your twenty?"

Trip Jones's deep voice came over the line. "Ninth-floor stairwell. The floors above me are clear. No sign of another bomb or any civilians or suspects in the building."

"Roger that. Continue your search." Captain Cutler wasted neither time nor words to keep his team moving in its symbiotic fashion. "Taylor, what's your twenty?"

Alex Taylor chimed in. "Third floor, working my way down, sir. Three through six are clear."

"All right, Murdock, I'm putting you to work."

Miranda snapped to attention at her captain's summons.

"I need you to leave your position and take over the search of the last two floors."

"Yes, sir."

"Here. Take this." Rafe handed her his big metal flashlight, then pulled a smaller spare from one of the pockets in his utility vest and stuck it between his teeth to free up his hands.

"Thanks, Sarge."

While she pulled her gun and checked the clip, the sergeant opened the carryall bag he'd brought with him and started gently packing the blocks of C-4 he could safely remove.

Captain Cutler was still issuing directions from the command center in the van. "Taylor, you're with me right now. I need you to take the box in to Sergeant Delgado."

"Roger that. Taylor out."

Quinn's steady voice sounded behind her. "Cutting the blue wire in three, two, one…"

Miranda held her breath and heard the tiny snip. No

boom. Always a good sign. She exhaled and headed for the door. "You two okay here?"

"Wait." She glanced back as Quinn put on his glasses and straightened. His laser-blue gaze reached her clear across the room and jolted through her. "Check on my daughter again."

She nodded and tapped her radio, beginning to understand the depths of how much a father could love his child, and just how much he would risk to keep her safe. "Captain? Do you have eyes on Fiona Gallagher?"

"She's right here in the van with me and Elise Brown." He chuckled, a rare sound. "I gave her a walkie-talkie without batteries to play with, and she's running her own op, copying nearly everything I say. Tell Quinn not to worry. She's occupied."

"Thank you, sir. Murdock out." She never took her eyes off Quinn. "Fiona's with the captain. She's just fine. I'll check her myself once I get out there, and radio in to the sergeant."

"Be safe," Quinn warned.

Miranda smiled. "Don't either of you blow up."

And then she was out the door and down the stairs to the second floor. The offices were smaller and more numerous here, belonging to paper pushers rather than researchers or executives. Leading with her flashlight and gun, hand over fist, she moved quickly along each hallway, meticulously checking in each and every door on the floor. She nudged open the door to the stairwell landing, looking up and down before venturing out. "Second floor clear."

She made her way down to the first floor, tuning out

most of the chatter on her headset. "KCPD," she announced with each new room she entered. Door open, light on, check behind desk, look inside closet. Close doors and move on. She ignored Christmas trees and Hanukkah decorations, paid little heed to whether the decor of each space was flashy or homey or modern. She was simply searching for bombs and bodies and hidden bad guys, making sure the citizens of Kansas City were out of harm's way.

She was doing her job, doing it well.

Until one of the captain's commands resonated loudly in her ear. "Kincaid, you're my eyes in the sky. Have you spotted anyone showing a particular interest in what's going on?"

Miranda pulled up short behind the reception desk in the GSS lobby. Eye in the sky. That was codespeak for when the sniper on the team found a high vantage point where she could take a clean shot or provide intel as needed for the rest of the team. *That* was *her* job. And Holden Kincaid was doing it.

You're not good enough.

The team can get the job done without you.

They don't really need you.

"Shut up." Miranda silently cursed that voice denigrating her in her head. She still had the same badge, the same skills she'd possessed when she joined SWAT. Had she been blind to her shortcomings before the RGK's blitz attack? Or had something in her truly changed that day?

"Murdock?" the captain questioned.

Oh, hell. Her mike was on. "Nothing, sir." *Shake it*

off. She literally shook her ponytail down her back and straightened her shoulders. "First floor clear."

"We've got your usual looky-loos, press vans and reporters lined up on the outer road leading to the interstate. It's pretty wide-open countryside to the west and south of the building." Holden Kincaid was back on the line. "Wait. I've got a black car parked in front of that trucking company about half a mile to the north beyond the cordoned-off perimeter. I count three men inside. They're separated from the rest of the crowd."

Black car? A different voice spoke inside Miranda's head. "Can you make out the plate number?" she asked.

Holden must be adjusting his binoculars because several seconds passed before he rattled it off.

Captain Cutler recognized the license number as soon as Miranda did. "The first three digits match the plate of that car with the camera creep outside Quinn's estate."

She remembered the name on the car rental agreement, too. It was the second black BMW an Alex Mostek had taken from one of the airport rental places. A man was entitled to like a certain kind of car, but she wasn't buying the coincidence of the same cars showing up near Quinn at two different locations three times in the same week, either.

Thank God he wasn't on a radio to hear of the suspect in the area. Quinn was working with enough C-4 to kill him, Sergeant Delgado and maybe the two other SWAT cops in the building if he got distracted and made a mistake.

The need to do her part to put an end to this nightmare got her moving. "I'm checking it out."

She was reluctantly grateful for Holden's next report. "Be advised you need to use the east exit and stick to the parking lots or he'll see you coming."

"Roger that."

Captain Cutler, of course, always had the last word. "We've got five minutes until I want that building clear, and I expect a roll call from every one of you, so make it fast."

"Yes, sir." Miranda raced to the side door leading out into the parking lot and pocketed the flashlight before stepping outside. A brisk wind chapped her cheeks, reminding her that her winter coat was still upstairs in Quinn's office. But five minutes, twelve flights of stairs and their first real lead on whoever was behind the threats to Fiona, Quinn and GSS forced her to ignore the cold and hunker down a bit to move forward at a good pace along the side of the building.

Once she left the shade of the building, she had to squint against the afternoon sunlight reflecting off the snowy hills around her. Once her eyes had adjusted to the brightness outside, she covered the distance across the parking lot and ran along the fenced lots between GSS and the next set of buildings in this industrial-park area. Her boots kept her feet warm and dry as she crunched through the snow, but her jeans were soaking in the moist cold and chilling the skin around her knees and calves.

"You're headed right for them," Holden advised. He was probably on the roof of one of these buildings already. "If you circle the truck company offices—the yellow brick facade—you'll come up on the car's backside."

"Roger that."

The cold was making her fingers stiff and she wished she'd at least stopped by the SWAT van to bag a pair of gloves. But determination was fueling her and the clock was ticking. If she could find out who was in the car, she might be able to put a stop to this dangerous game. She could protect the Gallaghers the way she knew how and prove to herself that she still had the mojo she needed to make it as a SWAT cop.

"Kincaid, I want you on the ground now to provide backup," the captain ordered.

Miranda paused at the corner of the building and leaned back against the bricks. Great. Just what she needed—the man poised to replace her on the team swooping down to save the day because Cutler didn't think she could do the job herself. While the rational part of her knew SWAT was all about teamwork, that raw need to prove she was worthy tried to get inside her head again.

She gritted her teeth to silence the voices of doubt and tried to fill her head with images of the dark-haired little girl who was depending on her, and the dark-haired father who was risking his own life to take a bomb apart so they could all be safe. Flexing her fingers around the grip of her Glock, Miranda took in one last steadying breath, nodded her own readiness and spun around the corner.

She spotted the target vehicle almost immediately

and darted between the semitruck trailers parked on the outer road behind it. She peeked out the far side to make sure she was in the car's blind spot and then crept up behind it, sticking close to the trucks and bending her legs to keep herself low to the ground. The plume of exhaust coming from the tailpipe told her the engine was running.

Were they curiosity seekers just trying to stay warm? Or was someone much more sinister preparing to make a quick getaway after seeing the results of his handiwork? Either way, she doubted Quinn would appreciate the obsession with him and his company.

"The briefcase is in the box," Sergeant Delgado reported in her ear. "Quinn got it down to a safer payload. We're moving it outside now to blow it."

"The parking lot is clear." The captain indicated they should bring the reinforced bomb box out to the deserted parking lot east of the building. "SWAT 1, sound off your twenty."

One by one, they reported by rank, ensuring every man on the team was safely accounted for before detonation. "Delgado, first floor. Exiting the building now."

"Jones, north entrance. Civilians are clear of the blast zone."

"Taylor, exiting the building now. Gallagher's with us."

Miranda opened her mouth to report in last, but another voice beat her to it.

"Kincaid. North of GSS, approaching Murdock on her three."

Was she part of this team or not?

"Murdock?" the captain prompted.

"Murdock here," she whispered, feeling her confidence sink like a stone. Maybe she should be grateful the captain had included her at all. *Keep it together.* This time she kept her voice low, since the wind would blow the sound straight at the car she was approaching. "I'm twenty yards behind the black car. Two men in the front seat. One in the back. I'm going in to get a look."

Determined to ignore Holden Kincaid's imminent arrival and deal with the potential threat herself, Miranda moved up onto the asphalt behind the car and silently angled herself around to get a look in the open window before she was spotted in one of the mirrors. Closer, closer. The man in the backseat was leaning toward the half-open window, clearly intent on the SWAT van, yellow cordon tape and news reporters and cameras gathered around the GSS building.

She quickly processed the details. Gray hair. Gaunt features. Curly gray beard. For a split second she envisioned an older, shaggier version of Nikolai Titov. But the man turned and saw her. Pale eyes. Not Nikolai.

"KCPD," she announced. "I need you to step out of the car. I just need to question you. Do it now."

The man thumped the seat in front of him and shouted in a foreign language. His window went up as the front window went down and a hand came out.

"Gun!" she shouted.

The car shifted into gear as the driver popped off two rounds in Miranda's direction. The engine growled and the back tires spun on the wet pavement.

Miranda quickly aimed as the car lurched forward. Her first shot took off the driver's side mirror. The front wheels found traction and the car fishtailed into a U-turn.

"Murdock!"

She stood her ground in the middle of the road and took out the right headlight. The passenger-side window went down and a second gun came out. She heard men shouting gibberish from the car—to her? To each other?—in a language she didn't understand.

More bullets peppered the pavement at her feet.

Miranda aimed for the front tire.

"Fire in the hole!"

The command in her ear distracted her for a split second and her shot pinged off the bumper.

The car picked up speed.

"Murdock! Move!"

Boom! The muffled report of the exploding box thundered through the cold air and shivered right down her spine. "Quinn?"

He'd better have been clear of that bomb.

"Murdock!" Holden Kincaid's voice dragged her back to the black car barreling toward her.

She raised her gun. But it was too close. It was too late to get off the shot.

The heat from the engine glanced off her body as she leaped out of the way. She landed hip first in the snow and rolled down into the ditch as the BMW blew past her. Pain burned along her forearm and throbbed in her knees and elbow by the time she cracked the ice at the bottom of the ditch and crashed to a stop.

Miranda heard two more shots, but they hadn't come from her. Somewhere in that roll down the hill, she'd lost her earpiece and weapon. The world of snow, trash and dead field grass reeled through her spinning vision as she pushed herself up to her hands and knees. And then two large hands were helping her to her feet and dragging her up to the road.

"Crazy lady." Holden Kincaid sat her down on the pavement and knelt in front of her "Cutler said you were fearless."

"Huh?" She blinked several times and breathed in the cold, crisp air, clearing her head and settling the queasy aftermath in her topsy-turvy stomach.

"Are you hit?" Kincaid's hands probed her arms and legs, searching for injuries.

"Ow!" Okay, so she must have scraped up her arm pretty good. But the vest had protected everything vital, and neither the bullets nor the car had actually struck her. "I'm fine."

Her cheek was burning now, too. Maybe that was just the cold, wet glop from the ditch clinging to her.

"How many fingers am I holding up?"

She pushed all three fingers away. "Enough to annoy me. Where's my gun?"

Holden put her Glock into her hand and then helped her to her feet. Miranda brushed aside any further assistance and surveyed the area. She didn't need to hear Holden reporting in to know the suspects were long gone. "The car got away, sir. Better call a bus. I think she's okay, but Murdock needs to be checked out." He covered his mike with a leather-gloved hand. "Can you walk?"

She batted his hand aside and stretched up on tiptoe to speak into his radio. "Cancel the ambulance, Captain. I'm scraped up, but I'm fine."

Holden grinned. "I'll take that as a yes. We're heading in, sir."

In a way, Holden Kincaid reminded Miranda a lot of her brother, John. Big man. Easy smile. Dry sense of humor. But she pressed her lips tight to hide the traitorous smile that wanted to answer him. She should not like this guy. He was the competition.

Besides, there was another man on her mind. A handsome father who'd kissed her in the midst of danger, who'd stuck by her side despite every effort to isolate herself with the danger of the bomb. A man whose image had gotten inside her head when she should have been focused on the car that tried to run her down. "Is everyone okay?" she asked.

"If you mean the bomb, yeah. The threat is neutralized and everyone's safe." Holden gestured down the road, and she fell into step beside him as they rejoined the team at the van. "I think you're the only one we need to worry about."

Miranda wiped the moisture and mud off her gun with shaky, numbing fingers before holstering it at her back. She'd missed her shot, gotten a stupid minor injury and was being escorted back to command by her replacement. Quinn and Sergeant Delgado had taken care of the bomb. Captain Cutler and Quinn's assistant had taken care of Fiona.

She'd fallen into the snow and mud and let the suspects shooting at her get away.

Way to shine, Murdock. Way to shine.

Miranda was bleeding.

Quinn tried to concentrate on the debriefing with Michael and his team up in his office, but all his brain could see at the moment was the blood oozing from the scrape on her cheek. Trip Jones had cut off the shredded sleeve of her sweater and blouse and packed a pressure bandage on the long gash on her forearm and elbow. But there were still broken and muddy reeds of grass stuck in her hair, and the graze on her cheek was bleeding.

This was *his* building, *his* problem. The threats were against *him*—destroy his company, take his daughter. He should be the one getting hurt—no one else. If he had known Miranda was going to be playing chicken with cars and guns, he would have insisted she stay with Fiona in the SWAT van. He would have kept her in his sight while he and Rafe cut apart that bomb and detonated what was left of it outside the building. He would have...

...not done any of those things, he admitted. He'd hired Miranda Murdock specifically because she was a woman who could handle bombs and bad guys and guns. She could think on her feet. Hell, she could think clearly enough when the pressure was on that she still had the time and energy to argue with him. Even now, while she was shivering in her damp clothes, just thirty minutes after the bomb had been detonated and the mystery car had sped off to the interstate and disappeared, she was clear-eyed and contributing to the sharing of facts after the incident. Michael Cutler expected her to be tough. *He* expected her to be tough, or he never would have hired her.

But that was the logic in his head talking. Something else, closer to his heart, something primal that was almost painful to acknowledge, wanted to do something about her getting hurt.

"I got a good look at the man in the backseat," she said.

Michael sat on the sofa across from Miranda. "Good. I'll have you sit down with a sketch artist at the Fourth Precinct. Today, if possible."

"The sooner, the better," she insisted. "I don't want to forget anything."

"You said they were speaking a foreign language? Any idea what it was?"

She twisted her hands together, trying to hide the way she was shivering. "Russian, maybe? Slavic? Like I said, there was a lot of noise and distraction."

All these grown men around the room, treating her like she was one of the guys, like she was just as impervious to pain as they had to be. Quinn had never considered himself particularly chivalric, but it made good common sense to drape his suit jacket around her shoulders to add an extra layer of warmth. He ignored her startled "Thank you." But he could feel the verdant gaze that tilted up and followed him all the way across the room to the bar sink where he wet a couple of paper towels with cool water.

Fiona was there in the kitchenette area at her little table and chairs, playing happily away with the walkie-talkie Michael had given her. "Woger that," she spoke into the mouthpiece, then held it up to Petra's ear, fortunately oblivious to the details of the adults' conversation and just what kind of danger she'd been in. "Mudock out."

Inwardly, he smiled. He was pretty fascinated by the nanny, too. Outwardly? He tried to keep it all cool, calm and collected. But he was quickly failing. He couldn't keep his eyes off the wound or her hair or the vulnerable extra tilt of her chin as she continued to answer questions.

Miranda clutched the jacket together at her neck when he returned. Seeing her in his coat, on his furniture, in his office—especially with other men in the room—tapped into something slightly more possessive than protective, and eased some of that raw, unsettling need to take care of her. Quinn perched on the edge of the sofa beside her. "Here." He dabbed away some of the mud and grit from around the scrape on her cheek, then pressed it against the seeping wound. "Did the men sound like Nikolai Titov?" he asked.

She hissed a breath of pain through her teeth before answering. "It was similar. I didn't understand what he and his associates were saying when they spoke in their native language here, either." Still stubbornly showing that streak of independence, she took the towels from his fingers and held them against her cheek herself. She turned the rest of her answer back to Michael. "Mr. Titov isn't the man I saw."

But Michael was looking at Quinn. "Where are Titov and his associates now?"

"I don't know. Once David came in, my only concern was the bomb and getting Fiona and the others out of the building. Where they went after that…?"

Quinn didn't realize that Elise had been tracking his movements across the office, too, until he caught her watching him with a curious frown from across the coffee table. She quickly looked away and crossed to where David Damiani stood near Quinn's desk. "They're gone. Nikolai took off with Louis pretty much as soon as David got us outside. I'm assuming he took them to their hotel. Would you like me to find out where they're staying?"

"Please," Michael answered. He gestured to Holden Kincaid, who opened the door for Elise and followed her out to her office.

Odd that Titov and his men had skipped out so quickly. Quinn had been certain that they'd had more argument to give about reopening the St. Feodor plant. Maybe, with their Eastern European background, they were cautious about the gathering of reporters outside, and being associated with any kind of attack that could be construed as a terrorist event.

Quinn was still thinking about the curious timing of men with foreign accents watching the building in crisis and shooting at Miranda, and the unexpected visit from Titov, when Rafe Delgado handed Michael a copy of the email Miranda had printed out. "We've got this photo and message about the bomb. But who was the first person to find the device? To actually put eyes on it? You, Quinn?"

David straightened from the back of the couch where he'd been sitting. "I can answer that." He circled around the end of the couch to face the senior officer. "Ozzie Chang, one of our computer geeks, found the email and called me in. I went into the lab myself and discovered it shortly after noon. That's when I called 911 and ordered the building evacuation."

"Where was Ozzie?" Quinn asked, rising to his feet. "He wasn't supposed to be working in the lab today."

David shook his head. "He was in his office when he called me."

"He called you because of the email, not because he'd found the bomb itself?"

"I guess." David's square jaw clenched before he cursed. "You think he could have put it there?"

"I'm not accusing one of my own people. With the holidays and a nearly deserted building, someone with the right skills could get inside." Although Quinn couldn't fathom how an outsider could get into one of GSS's most secure rooms, he didn't want to think that the easiest answer was that someone he knew and trusted was behind these threats. Still, Ozzie did have the know-how to hack into GSS from a remote location. The question was why. "I'm just trying to make sense of something that doesn't make sense to me. He did come in to help me yesterday, but I sent him on vacation for the rest of the week. What was he doing here?"

Miranda huddled inside his jacket as she stood beside Quinn. "Does Ozzie know how to build a bomb?"

"I hire very smart people to work for me. Anything's possible." He still wasn't buying it. "But what's his motive?"

"Two and a half million dollars?" David suggested.

"The money's already been paid. Why risk killing more innocent people and doing millions of dollars' worth of damage?"

"Maybe he was covering his tracks."

Quinn raked his fingers through his hair and rubbed at the headache forming at the base of his skull. "This feels personal, not like it's about the money."

"I wouldn't write off the computer geek yet." David braced his hands at his hips and puffed up, refusing to have his idea dismissed. "There's one more thing, boss. Whoever put the bomb there used an authorized access code. Nothing was flagged to security when the door opened."

"Could that code be what the hacker was after?" Miranda asked.

"Or maybe Ozzie punched it in himself." David's point was made, even if Quinn didn't like the idea of a traitor working for him.

Michael Cutler stood and signaled to his men. "Taylor. Trip. Grab Kincaid and go find this Ozzie Chang. And let's get some detectives to look into his financials. Mr. Damiani, can you get us an address?"

"I can take you there myself." David nodded and headed out the door with the uniformed cops on his heels.

"Rafe and I will make sure your assistant and the three of you get home safely." SWAT Team 1 was on the move again. "Chang either saw that bomb and lied to your security chief, or someone used the code to get in after he left and we need him to narrow down the time frame when that could have happened—"

"—or Ozzie has a lot of explaining to do about his loyalty to me and GSS." Quinn was running through the same possibilities Michael was, and was ready to find some answers. He went to the kitchenette and scooped Fiona up into his arms.

Miranda was already gathering up their coats. "No matter what, I have a feeling there are a couple of detectives who'll want to question Ozzie."

"Forget the detectives." Quinn intended to take the women home and then accompany Michael and his men. "I want to talk to him myself."

"I AM ONE STEP AHEAD OF YOU, Quinn Gallagher." The figure sitting in the car laughed. The brilliant self-made man thought he could plan for every situation, that he could control every outcome with his brains or money or business savvy. "Look who has control now."

The child would have been so easy to take while the big boss of Gallagher Security Systems was playing hero. As suspected, Quinn wouldn't be able to resist tackling the bomb himself, once he recognized bits and pieces of his own designs all set into place to topple his empire. Quinn was the type of man to step up and take responsibility, to look out for those around him, to notice who needed him and who deserved his help.

He was a born leader, a consummate protector—in every single facet of his life and work. Except one.

And that one mistake, that one oversight—that one glaring example of Quinn Gallagher not giving a damn about the right person—was the reason for being here.

The figure sitting behind the wheel clutched at the pain stabbing straight through the heart. No one should have to suffer that kind of loss. No one should have to feel that helpless—to know everything one tried to get noticed, to make things right, wasn't enough.

There was only one way to make things right now.

Quinn Gallagher had to suffer in the very same way.

Remembering the success of the day, the driver sat up squarely behind the wheel. Everyone was packing up now. Catching their breaths. Escorting people home. Crisis averted. Now Quinn would go back to his mansion and seclude himself with his thoughts. He'd reflect on every misstep and close call of the past four days, wondering what he'd missed, whom he'd offended, where he'd gone wrong. He thought he could fix this if he surrounded himself with the right people and thought about the game long enough and hard enough.

It was a delight to watch him be confused, angry—to watch the great Quinn Gallagher not have all the answers.

There were so many delicious ways this afternoon could have gone. Property damage. Destruction of the GSS mainframe computer. Loss of lives. Losing the young life most important to Quinn.

But the timing wasn't right. The game had to be played a certain way, on a certain schedule—mimicking the time frame of the driver's own suffering—or the satisfaction that was so long overdue wouldn't be gratifying enough.

It was the only way to make things right.

Paying little heed to the police officers still working around the GSS building, the figure behind the wheel speed-dialed the mercenary who'd been paid very well to do exactly as ordered. "Is it done?"

"It's done."

"Good." The boss picked up the disposable phone on the dashboard and ripped open the package. "Then I'll send my next message."

Chapter Ten

"Did he have family?" Michael Cutler asked.

Quinn's eyes burned as he tore his gaze away from the neat bullet hole in the middle of Ozzie Chang's forehead and looked across the body on the floor to his friend. "Parents in San Francisco. I'd better call them."

"Let the detectives handle it." Michael braced his hands on his knees and pushed himself away from the puddle of blood on the entryway's hardwood floor. "Why don't you take Randy and Fiona home? You all need some rest."

"I can't rest until I find out who's behind this, Michael." He curled his fingers into fists at his side. "Ozzie was barely out of college. Those guards at the Kalahari plant had no clue what hit them. Men are watching my house and my daughter and shooting at Miranda. I need to figure this out. I need to get ahead of this guy and stop him." He raked his fingers through his hair in frustration and came back shaking another fist. "That's what I do, Michael. I find solutions to problems. I solve puzzles that other people can't. I figure things out."

"Don't beat yourself up, buddy." Michael literally took Quinn by the arm and led him to the front door. "That's part of what this guy wants from you. He wants you out of your element. He wants you to suffer."

"He's doing a damn fine job. My God..." A horrendous thought hit him, one that almost made him gag as he turned back to the grisly murder. "What if that was Fiona?" He sought out Michael's steady gaze, needing someone, anyone, to understand. "I will die—I will kill—before I let something like this happen to my little girl."

He circled around the body to look into the sparsely furnished living room of Ozzie's small white house. A beat-up sofa, a new recliner and a wall full of electronics—gaming systems, a large flat-screen TV, computer towers. Not a lot to show for twenty-some years of life. Yet Quinn had envied the young man just yesterday.

Ozzie Chang had been young and full of fun and possibilities. He'd come in to GSS during his vacation at Quinn's request. A bullet to the head was his punishment for helping him.

Or was it his payment for helping someone else?

Quinn scrubbed his fingers over the five o'clock shadow on his jaw. "How soon before the detectives and CSIs get here and get us some answers?" The rage and grief cleared a small corner of his brain and gave him a chance to observe and think. "Oz must have known whoever he let in the door—or else didn't feel threatened by his killer. There's no sign of a struggle."

"Quinn—"

"Do you think the people who paid him to hack into GSS and deliver a bomb betrayed him to cover the connection to them? Didn't he know how much money I have? How much money I'd pay to ensure the safety of the people I care about?"

"You think Chang hacked your system? That he was a mole in your company?"

"It sure seems like somebody is." Quinn tamped down on the emotions raging through his blood and tried to present a logical argument. "Or is Ozzie the innocent kid I thought he was, and he stumbled onto something he shouldn't in the lab? He saw something in the computers, or he saw someone place that bomb—and now he's another innocent victim in this retribution game."

Betrayal or a friend caught in the cross fire?

He didn't like either option.

Quinn faced Michael again, counting off options on his fingers. "I've been racking my brain, trying to come up with suspects—people who might hold a serious grudge against me. Mom's live-in boyfriend, who I threw out of the house once I was big enough and tough enough to get him to stop hitting her. Business competitors. I've absorbed several companies around the world into GSS and have put others completely out of business."

"Quinn, stop. You're grasping at straws."

"I have to grasp at something! I can't stand not being in control. I hate it."

"I know where you're coming from. When my Jillian had a stalker, before I married her, I was... When he had her tied up with a gun to her head, I..." Quinn saw the first crack of emotion in Michael's stern facade. "It was the first time in a long time that I was truly scared. And I didn't like it. It threw me off my game and I almost lost her." He swallowed hard, glanced away for a moment, then looked him right in the eyes. "You and I are a lot alike, my friend. The bad guys don't get to win. But you're in no shape to do battle right now. You're exhausted. Your anger is getting in the way. And this is not the place where you want to do your thinking." Michael went to the front door and opened it. "So go home and get some rest."

Quinn glanced down at the injustice of the body at their feet. "And give that bastard the chance to do this to somebody else because of me?"

"Think of it this way—a few hours' sleep will clear your mind so you *can* figure it out." Michael rarely talked about the man who had stalked and kidnapped his wife. The glimpse of deep, conflicted emotion from his normally unflappable friend made Quinn understand that Michael truly got what he was going through.

It also gave him hope that he could get through this crisis, too. As long as he kept his head. "I guess I'll wind up with a cranky toddler if I don't get Fiona to bed."

"And, I've entrusted you with one of my team, Quinn. Randy's not as tough on the inside as she is on the outside. I need you to take good care of her."

Quinn looked through the open doorway to see a battered Miranda standing guard over the car where his daughter slept. Her eyes were sharp as she paced up and down the sidewalk. But the mark on her face was already bruising, and she hugged her arms around her middle as she walked, as though not even the hat and coat she wore were enough to keep her warm.

Those same possessive, protective instincts he'd discovered in his office this afternoon heated his blood. Yeah, he could take care of Miranda, too. If she'd let him.

"All right." Maybe he could do more good for the cops, his company and those two women outside if he could get some rest and some rational thoughts in his head. He extended his hand to Michael to thank him for all he and his team had done for him today. "But call me the minute KCPD has anything to report."

"Will do."

"Captain?" Trip Jones called them back into the living room. "I pulled this up on Chang's computer. You're going to want to see this."

Quinn should have walked on out the door.

The words typed on the screen were in big, bold print. The taunting promise in the words was even bigger.

> *I am one step ahead of you. Now Mr. Chang will never reveal the favor he did for me. Now you see I can get to you at work. I will require another 2.5 million in the Swiss account or I will strike much closer to home.*

"You got this, David?" The pictures on the wall of monitors in the estate's security command center were blurring.

Quinn was a weary man. He pulled off his glasses and scrubbed his hand over his entire face, from his aching eyes down to the sandpapery stubble of late-night beard growth on his jaw.

"Yes, sir." David Damiani's tie was loose, his suit jacket was draped over the back of the chair beside Quinn's and his coffee mug was nearly empty. "Between my men at the gate and Cutler's men doing periodic drive-bys, as well as me in the security office and Murdock upstairs, we're completely secure. I've got eyes on the front door, back door, side entrance and more. If our presence and technology aren't deterrent enough, at least there's no way we won't see this guy coming."

Quinn slipped his glasses back on to get a good look at the camera shots where David was pointing. He knew David's ego had probably taken a few dings the past few days. GSS employees had been killed. A bomb had been rigged in GSS headquarters. Quinn had called on his friend Michael Cutler and SWAT Team 1 in addition to David's private security team—not because Quinn doubted David could handle the threats, but because Quinn could never feel secure enough where Fiona was concerned.

It was hard to fight an enemy you couldn't see or identify, and Quinn knew the situation would be even more impossible if his security chief wasn't on the payroll. "I appreciate you coming in to take charge of watching over the house tonight. I know it's not your primary responsibility, but—"

"*You* are my responsibility, sir. Without you, GSS

falls apart." His big shoulders lifted with a shrug and a grin. "I'm thinking I'd be out of a job if something happened to you."

Quinn managed half a laugh at the wry humor. He motioned David to stay seated when he stood, then reached over to shake his hand. "Thanks. I'm turning in. If you need anything…"

"I won't. Good night, sir."

"Good night, David."

Quinn climbed the stairs to the main floor, taking note of every locked window and hallway camera in the silent house. Even though David had done the same an hour ago, Quinn checked the front door, the garage exit and mud room door before dragging his feet up the next set of carpeted stairs to the living quarters there.

More than the promise of his own bed and a few hours of sleep, the dim light shining into the hallway from Fiona's room drew him like a guiding beacon.

He paused in the doorway, leaned his head against the jamb and smiled at the scene inside. He wasn't the only one exhausted by the day.

Fiona sat in Miranda's lap in the rocking chair. Her cheek was smushed against Miranda's red pajama top, her bow-shaped mouth was slightly parted and her eyes were closed in sleep.

But what caught his heart and made him smile was the beautiful contrast of Miranda's golden hair hanging straight and loose and tangling with Fiona's dark curls. The book they'd been reading had fallen to the floor. Miranda's undamaged cheek rested against the crown of Fiona's hair and she was softly snoring right along with her.

Michael had charged him with taking care of both of these girls, but it was a task nobody had to ask of him. Feeling oddly energized and renewed by the endearing sight, despite the fatigue screaming from every cell of his body, Quinn tiptoed into the room. He picked up the book and set it aside, then slid his arms beneath Miranda's knees and around her back.

Miranda startled awake at his touch. "I should go..."

"Shh." Quinn whispered a reassurance and lifted them both from the chair. "Let me. Got her?"

Nodding, she tightened her arms around Fiona, who never stirred. With Miranda's help, he pulled back the covers and laid them both on the bed.

"She's content with you holding her." Quinn pulled the sheet and comforter up over them both and tucked them in. He caressed Fiona's hair, then bent to give her a kiss. "I don't want to wake her."

"I'll stay with her," Miranda promised, gently stroking Fiona's dark hair off her rosy cheeks.

He stayed where he was, hovering over the bed. He mimicked the same tender gesture, brushing Miranda's hair, still damp from her shower, away from her bruised cheek. Her green eyes were hooded, drowsy, fixed on his as he leaned in to kiss her temple, as well. "Good night, Miranda."

But her hand snaked out from beneath the covers to capture his jaw and guide his mouth down to hers instead. He gladly obliged the bold request, covering her lips with his, parting them. He slipped his tongue inside for a taste of her heat. He welcomed the answering pull of her lips beneath his, braced his hand against the headboard and leaned over farther to angle his mouth more completely over hers. A slow, liquid warmth ignited in his chest and seeped into his blood, giving life to his tired body, reminding him he was a strong, healthy man. But the hour was late, and with his daughter here there was little he could do about the aching needs this woman kindled inside him.

So with a deep breath and a troubled heart, he pulled away. But as long as those beautiful eyes were on him, he couldn't completely retreat. He'd wanted Miranda to bond with his daughter, and she had. But he was forming a bond with her, too. Her fingers brushed across his jaw; her thumb stroked his lips. She blinked her eyes and smiled. "Good night, Quinn."

When her eyes blinked shut with fatigue and didn't open again, he finally moved away. He set the storybook back in its place on the bookshelf, turned off the lamp and headed for the door. But he couldn't leave.

Everything he loved—everything he wanted— everything that truly mattered was sleeping in that bed behind him.

Even with guards and cameras and the holstered gun on top of the bookshelf, he couldn't be sure they were safe. His bedroom at the end of the hall was too far away. With Fiona and Miranda out of his sight, he wouldn't be able to relax.

So he kicked off his shoes and settled into the rocking chair beside the bed to watch them sleep. He wasn't leaving Miranda and Fiona tonight, not even for a moment.

But after half an hour of dozing fits and starts, Quinn woke again. Even this chair was too far away to assuage his loneliness and his need to protect this makeshift family. In his mind, there was only one logical thing he could do.

He got up and circled the double bed, pulling off his belt and untucking his shirt. And then he climbed into bed with them, stretching out on top of the covers behind Miranda.

Her back and bottom fit perfectly against his chest and groin. When she nestled against him in her sleep, he buried his nose in Miranda's thick, damp hair, filling his head up with the smells of sweet coconut and tangy citrus. She was warmth and health and life and every good thing he wanted in this world.

Quinn wrapped his arms around both of them and finally drifted off to sleep.

Chapter Eleven

2 Days until Midnight, New Year's Eve

Miranda wiped Fiona's sticky fingers and held the chair while the little girl climbed down and hurried to the end of the table to get Petra down from her seat.

After popping the last uneaten bite of Fiona's peanut-butter sandwich into her mouth, Miranda carried her cup and plate to the sink, where she rinsed them and stacked them in the dishwasher. Two successful meals under her belt now without trashing the kitchen. She sincerely hoped Quinn didn't mind ordering take-out pizza for dinner because the cook wasn't scheduled to be back until after the New Year, and she'd already discovered a dearth of anything microwaveable in this house except for popcorn.

She wondered if the Marines would mind if she called her brother again to get a recipe for dinner. Thinking of John and how amused he'd be at her quandary made her smile. "Probably not."

It was amazing how a little success in the nannying department, a fresh bandage for the cut on her forearm and a good night's sleep could refresh her energy and boost her confidence in her responsibilities here. Miranda had never considered herself a domestic-bliss kind of woman before, but waking up with an aroused man hugged tightly to her backside and a little girl sprawled with innocent abandon on the pillow next to hers gave her ideas about wanting to give the cooking and cleaning and "welcome home, honey" routine a try.

This morning, for the first time in months, she hadn't felt alone when she woke up. And it wasn't just the physical closeness of having an extra body in the bed. There was something incredibly sensuous and equally tender about waking with Quinn's hand splayed possessively on the flat of her stomach, then feeling his lips nuzzle the sensitive skin at her nape before he whispered, "Good morning."

"Good morning. Sleep well?"

The sandpapery stubble of his beard was like the caress of a cat's tongue when he nodded against her neck and answered, "Best sleep I've had in years." His hold around her tightened like a hug and she knew he was looking beyond her to the child sleeping several inches away. "They're perfect angels when they're asleep, aren't they?"

Miranda had laced her fingers with Quinn's and marveled at how well their hands fit together, how well their bodies fit, how well their thoughts meshed. She was warm, contented. She had the idea that this was where she belonged, *this* was where she finally fit in. And if she was only dreaming it, she didn't want to wake up. It had been easy to agree on Fiona's beauty and so much more. "Perfect."

"Petwa and I help."

And then there was reality and the bright sunlight of a cold winter's day.

Miranda heard the scratch of a step stool sliding across the tile floor and felt the tug at the sleeve of her insulated henley shirt. Quinn had sequestered himself in his home office right after breakfast and she hadn't seen him since. And, once again, she had a dark-haired girl at her elbow. As had quickly become a habit with nearly every task, Fiona joined her at the sink, wanting to help with the grown-up's job.

"Okay. Set Petra down so she doesn't get wet." The doll dropped to the floor immediately and Fiona reached for the glass Miranda had used. In a deft move she hoped the girl was still too young to notice, she pulled her plastic cup back out of the dishwasher and switched it with the breakable glass.

They were both wet to their elbows and kneeling in front of the open dishwasher door to load the cube of dishwasher soap when the kitchen door swung open and Quinn strode inside. "Hello?"

"Over here." Miranda popped up from behind the counter.

Fiona batted her hand away when Miranda automatically reached back to start the machine. "I push the button," she insisted.

"This one here," Miranda pointed out. Fiona pushed the button and smiled from pigtail to pigtail when the wash cycle started right up.

"Look what I did, Daddy." Fiona hugged her father's leg and tilted her face all the way back to look up at him. "I did the dishes. And Wandy helped."

Miranda grinned at the mention. The five-minute task had taken fifteen, but she'd stayed busy and Fiona had been entertained. Quinn cupped her head and congratulated her before sending her off to play on her own for a few minutes. "Good job, sweetie. Why don't you go up to your room and help Petra try on some of the new outfits she got for Christmas? I need to talk to Miranda, okay?"

"Okay."

Quinn turned to watch her push through the swinging door and listen for the light rhythm of footsteps going up the stairs, giving Miranda the chance to notice the scuffs of dust on the sleeve of his navy blue sweater and the knees of his corduroy slacks. When he faced her again, she plucked a cobweb from his hair and took the liberty of smoothing that stray lock on his forehead back into place. "Where have you been?"

He adjusted his glasses in that adorably nerdy habit of his. "Up in the attic, going through some boxes of Val's things."

Oh. The late wife. Nothing like the mention of the woman he'd loved and married and started a family with to put a crimp in that silly dream of belonging here. She was the nanny. The bodyguard. Not the future Mrs. Gallagher. Miranda brushed away the cobweb and the feel of his silky hair against her fingers on the leg of her jeans.

"Looking for something in particular?" she asked,

matching her posture to the businesslike tone of his voice.

He spread a piece of paper with a computer-generated picture on top of the center island. "This is the police artist's rendering of the guy in the backseat of that black BMW that Michael faxed over from KCPD this morning." He set an old black-and-white photograph on the counter beside it and tapped at the faded image. "Is this the man you saw in the car that tried to run you down?"

Miranda picked up the photograph. She didn't need to see the drawing because those pale eyes and gaunt features shouting some kind of warning to the men in the front seat of the car bearing down on her were embedded clearly in her memory.

She studied the image of a young man in his late twenties. His hair was curly, dark. The swim trunks he wore revealed a muscular upper body. But the eyes looking straight into the camera were the same.

"Gray up his hair, put some wrinkles on him and shave off about fifty pounds, and yes, that's the man I saw." She set the picture back on the counter and frowned. "Who is it?"

"Vasily Gordeeva. My father-in-law."

The silence that filled the kitchen following that announcement left Miranda fidgeting inside her skin. Quinn could stand there and bore holes into the photograph with those laser-blue eyes for as long as he wanted to process whatever thoughts were going on inside his head. But she needed to move.

Spying the coffeemaker, and inhaling a whiff of the

fragrant roasted liquid, she went to the cabinet above it and pulled down a mug to pour herself a cup. She held up the pot toward Quinn and he looked up long enough to nod.

Some of the tension in him had eased by the time she rejoined him at the island and handed him his drink. "Thanks."

Miranda cradled her mug between her hands to warm her fingers. "Do you and your wife's family not get along?"

"I've never met the man." Another cryptic statement, punctuated with a swallow of coffee. "Val left Lukinburg when she was six or seven. Neither she nor her mother ever had contact with him again."

Now she was getting an idea of where his thoughts had been. "So why would your father-in-law be spying on you?"

"And why would he want to hurt the grandchild he's never even met?"

More to the point, "How could he? I thought he was in prison."

"So did I."

Miranda set down her mug and lined up the two images side by side on the counter. "You know, there's a big difference between this strapping young man and the elderly gentleman I saw."

"A gentleman wouldn't plant bombs or take potshots at you."

"Technically, he wasn't the one doing the shooting."

"Small comfort."

Miranda appreciated the sarcasm on her behalf. But

there had to be an explanation somewhere. "What if he's ill? He wouldn't be the first long-term prisoner to be released near the end of his sentence because of health issues."

Quinn shot his fingers through his hair, destroying the tidying up she'd done earlier. "And his first wish as a free man is to come after me? He doesn't need the money. I'm guessing he had to pay a hefty fee to somebody to leave the country, maybe even to get out of prison. He's rented multiple luxury cars here."

"All three men were wearing suits and ties and nice wool coats," she added.

"And goons with guns and cameras don't come cheap."

"You said he was imprisoned for his politics?"

Quinn picked up her mug and carried both of them to the sink. "Specifically, he was put away for raising funds and running the campaign for a presidential candidate who turned out to be the front man for a Lukinburger mob boss. According to Val, the guy won. But shortly after, there was a revolution and the mob-influenced government was overthrown, and Vasily went to prison."

"And neither you nor your wife were ever any part of that?"

Quinn shook his head. "Val was embarrassed by his criminal connections, I think. They certainly put her and her mother in danger after the revolution there. So no, once they became American citizens, they were never part of anything there."

Great. So they could finally name a suspect, but he lacked a motive.

They stood side by side at the counter, staring at the contrasting images of Vasily Gordeeva.

"I was thinking," she started, reaching up to lift her ponytail and play with it for a few moments while her idea settled into place.

"About what?"

"The threat at Ozzie Chang's house."

Quinn pulled her ponytail from her fingers and smoothed it down the center of her back. "Let's try to forget it for a few hours, okay?"

As much as she wanted to savor the comforting caress, she turned to face him instead. "You think that message means he's coming here to the house, too, right?"

"Yes. He wants more money or 'I will strike much closer to home,'" he quoted.

Miranda narrowed her gaze on Quinn. "Well, hasn't he already been here?"

"Hmm?" For a smart man, this particular puzzle wasn't yet falling into place.

"The men in the car watching the house. The guy who took pictures of Fiona." Miranda reached for his hands, squeezing them between hers, willing him to understand. "If he's already been here, then a note like that doesn't make sense."

Quinn connected the dots with her, and maybe deduced a little something more. "There are two things going on here. And, just maybe, they're related."

"You've figured out who's behind this?"

"Partly." He pulled her hands to his lips and kissed her fingers. He was energized again, moving, on his way out the door. "I want to put in a call to my father-in-law first."

"WHY DON'T YOU BAKE COOKIES together?" Such an innocent suggestion for a wintry vacation evening.

But Miranda would rather run a timed simulation at the KCPD firing range.

Still, fearful of taking Fiona outside again in the darkness of twilight, even with lights blazing all around the house, she'd needed something to do to keep the little girl entertained. The last nanny, or maybe two or three nannies ago—the exact details had been blanked out by the momentary panic attack she'd had at Quinn's suggestion—had made great strides teaching Fiona the child-appropriate basics of cookie making. Cutting out shapes. Decorating them with sprinkles. Eating them.

Unfortunately, those were the same skills Miranda was familiar with when it came to baking.

And now their first batch was coming out of the oven. The edges were burned, the middles were doughy. Fiona waited on her step stool, ready to shake the colored-sugar bottles and chocolatey bits over their creations. Miranda checked the picture in the cookbook one more time to confirm that what she had in her oven mitt was a tray full of chewy hockey pucks rather than anything resembling sugar cookies.

But hopefully, as she scraped them off the cookie sheet and set them on the cooling rack, this exercise in frustration was more about the fun Fiona was having and less about Miranda's ability to produce something edible and appetizing.

"There you go, sweetie." She tested some of the hockey pucks that were cool enough to handle and set them on the plate in front of Fiona. "Have at it. Make them pretty."

While sugar and sprinkles flew, Miranda scooped up more cookie dough, trying to make the second tray more even in size. She double-checked the temperature of the oven one more time and slipped them inside.

The kitchen door swung open behind her. "Mmm. Smells good in here."

"Daddy! Look what we made."

Miranda wondered at her own little flutter of excitement at seeing Quinn walk into the room. Fiona jumped down from her step stool and trotted over to greet him, leaving a trail of green and red sugar in her wake.

She might as well admit the disaster this was right now. "Well, cleaning up this mess will certainly give us plenty to do between now and bedtime." She tossed her oven mitts on the counter. "Fair warning."

"About what?" Quinn scooped Fiona up in his arms and took a bite of the cookie she stuffed into his mouth. But it was clearly a struggle to get down. "I see. Got a glass of milk?"

"Coming right up."

Quinn set Fiona on the far edge of the counter and did his duty as a good father to eat the entire cookie and give her a wink as though he was enjoying it. Once he'd cleared his throat by downing half a glass of milk, he placed three cookies on a plastic plate and sent his daughter on a mission.

As soon as she was out the door and marching down the hallway, Quinn pressed the intercom button to call down to the men in the security command room. "David?"

"Sir?" the security answered back through a buzz of static.

"No emergency," Quinn assured him. "I'm sending my daughter down to you with a plate of cookies." Miranda laughed at the helpless face he made before speaking again. "Be nice and try one before you send her back. And remember, I pay you a lot of money."

"Okay…? I'll keep an eye out for her. Damiani out."

Quinn laughed with her as he came back to the center island to finish off his milk. "You weren't kidding when you said baking wasn't a strength of yours." He nodded toward the swinging door. "But that's one happy little girl."

"I guess I had fun, too. Can't say I'm proud of the results, but it's like a science experiment. And I liked my chemistry class in high school." Miranda gathered up the bowls and measuring cups scattered over the counter and carried them to the sink. "So how did your phone call with Elise Brown go? Did she get a hold of Nikolai Titov?"

Quinn joined her at the sink with another load of dirty dishes. "Yeah, I guess he took her out to dinner. I can't tell if Titov is trying to steal away the most organized member of my staff or if they're actually sweet on each other."

"Really?" Miranda ran the water until it got hot, and then she squirted in some liquid soap to wash the items by hand. "I'm no expert on such things, but I got the idea that Elise was sweet on you. She didn't seem real thrilled that you gave me your jacket and took care of me after the shooting outside your office."

"You noticed I was trying to take care of you, hmm?"

"I notice everything you do." Like the tender caresses he gave his daughter. The quizzical frowns he often gave her. The heated debates. The subtle, certain touches of his fingers or lips against her skin. The way he generated a heat that leaped between them whenever they were close, even standing side by side in front of the kitchen sink.

Quinn cleared his throat beside her, as if he still had a bite of that cookie stuck there. She had no such excuse for the difficulty she suddenly seemed to have catching her breath.

"Let me." Quinn nodded at the bandage on her arm and rolled up his shirtsleeves to plunge his hands into the sudsy water himself. "I think Elise is just protective of me. More mother hen than sweetheart. I count on her to make me look good to my clients and the people who work for me, especially when I'm stuck in my head with an idea or a business plan. She apparently smoothed things over with Titov. At least for the time being. Those kinds of people skills are invaluable to me as a businessman."

"She's a pretty woman, too." Miranda wet a second

dishrag to wipe down the counters and put some clear-thinking space between them while he washed.

"You're the second person to tell me that this week. I guess I've noticed in some part of my mind that she's attractive. But she must not be my type."

"So…" The bell on the oven went off and Miranda took out the last batch of cookies and set them on the cooling rack. At least they weren't burned. It was enough of a victory that she dared to ask, "What is your type?"

When she turned around, Quinn was right there, his thighs crowding hers back against the island as he set his soapy hands on the countertop on either side of her. "I think you know."

She definitely noticed the heat between them.

And the laser focus of those deep blue eyes skimming over her face.

She noticed the enticing wave of dark hair tumbling over his forehead, and the breadth of those shoulders straining beneath blue-striped oxford cloth as he leaned in.

She noticed the simple, masculine smells of soap and spice on his skin.

And she noticed the warm, gentle pressure of his fingertip brushing across her cheekbone.

"Me?" she uttered on a breathless whisper.

He held up the white-tipped finger.

Her hand flew to her cheek, which felt ridiculously hot. Oh, no. She had flour on her face.

Instead of answering with a word, he dropped his

gaze lower, to her left breast and the smudge of flour smeared there. He liked klutzy incompetents?

But the joke sounded lame, even inside her own head.

Quinn wasn't laughing. He looked serious, intent... hungry.

Her breath hissed when he brushed that same finger across the streak of flour—deliberately caressing the nubby weave of her shirt, the smooth satin of her bra, the shallow curve of her breast.

Miranda noticed the rapid tempo of her heart, racing beneath his touch. She noticed the way her tender nipple beaded to attention, straining to feel his touch there, as well.

She noticed his mouth moving toward hers, her lips parting in anticipation. His deep-pitched whisper was a husky caress against her ear. "You."

And then he was kissing her. Wanting her. Claiming her. His tongue swept along the needy swell of her lower lip and plunged inside her mouth to brand her with his sugar-cookie flavor and his abundant heat.

Miranda wound her arms around his neck, rubbing the aching tips of her breasts against the wall of his chest as she pulled herself up onto her toes to take everything he would give her. "Quinn." She clutched at the silk of his hair, nipped at his chin. "Quinn." She dragged her sensitive palms along the stubble of his jaw and down the column of his neck. She slipped her fingers beneath his collar, unhooked a button and slid her fingers beneath the crisp material to find warm, sleek skin. "Quinn."

"I know." He lifted her onto the countertop, spread her thighs and pulled her to the edge, holding her taut and open against his swelling desire. "I know."

Miranda's legs convulsed around his hips at the hard, intimate contact. She felt heavy, molten, weepy inside. She tried to think of reasons why they should stop. Fiona, others in the house. She worked for Quinn. He was the boss. A frustrating, intriguing, compassionate, sexy boss. "Are we crazy?"

"Yes." He slid his palms beneath the hem of her shirt, his strong hands sweeping hot and needy over the cool skin of her back. "It makes no sense." He yanked her shirt up, exposing her torso to the chilly air. "This makes no sense." He dipped his head and closed his hot mouth over the distended peak of her breast, wetting her through the thin material of her bra, laving her, catching the tip between his teeth and tongue until she let out a breathless gasp of torture and joy. "It's never been like this for me." He slid his fingers beneath her bottom and squeezed, lifted, showed her exactly what he wanted if there weren't layers of clothes between them. "I haven't figured you out yet."

Miranda clung to his shoulders and gasped against his neck. "Is that important?"

"It's a—"

The loud *whoop-whoop* of an alarm stopped Quinn midsentence, and Miranda froze against him. Emergency lights at the mud room door flashed on and off. For the longest of seconds she couldn't make out anything but the thundering of her pulse inside her ears.

Fiona shrieked from somewhere in the house.

"Loud noises." Miranda was pushing even as Quinn was pulling away.

"Fiona!" he shouted.

"She hates loud noises." She was jumping as Quinn lifted her off the counter. They straightened their clothes, ran toward the swinging door, forgot their own unanswered desires because a terrified little girl needed them right now. "Fiona!"

Like a chain-reaction crash on the highway, Miranda's senses slammed into place one by one. Security alarm. Intruders on the premises. Draw gun. Find Fiona.

Quinn saw her first, standing in the hallway— screaming, crying. He scooped her up in his arms and hugged her tight to his chest. "It's okay, baby. Daddy's got you. It's okay."

Another light flashed on and off at the front door. The alarm blared its warning.

Her own heart crying at Fiona's terror, Miranda brushed a dark curl off the little girl's cheek. "You'll be fine, sweetie. Daddy won't let go and I'll keep you safe."

Just as quickly as the compassion had welled up inside her, Miranda squashed it back down. She had one job to do, and this was it. She moved her hand from Fiona's head to Quinn's shoulder and urged him to come with her. "We need to get to one of the panic rooms."

He nodded, cradled Fiona's head against his shoulder and hurried toward the stairs.

A stampede of footsteps charged up the stairs from the lower level behind them.

"Keep moving," she ordered, pushing Quinn up the stairs. Miranda whirled around, her Glock gripped between her hands, and changed course to meet the approaching threat head-on.

She saw the end of a rifle first, appearing around the corner. She ducked into the nearest doorway and shouted, "KCPD! Halt right there!"

"Whoa!" A man in a dark uniform threw up his hands before he ever reached the hallway.

A second man stumbled into him. He pointed his gun up into the air and raised his hands, as well. "Murdock?"

"Holmes? Rowley?" These two bozos were running through the house, armed with assault rifles? She lowered her gun to a less lethal angle, but refused to lower her guard. "What's going on?"

"The black Beemer's here again," Holmes reported. "Three men inside."

"Here?"

"Two of your SWAT guys caught them at the gate and are bringing them in."

All at once the alarm stopped and David Damiani came up the stairs, speaking into his walkie-talkie. "Make sure you disarm them. Check for ankle holsters, knives and any other easy-to-hide weapons."

"Roger that." She recognized Sergeant Delgado's voice on the radio.

"Quinn!" Ignoring her gun and her authority and shouting for the boss, David pushed Rowley aside and glared down at her as he walked past. "Loose cannon," he muttered, signaling his men to fall in behind them. Then, in a louder voice, he announced, "Dirty Harriet here almost shot my boys."

"What?" She spun around to find Quinn standing on the bottom step. Wasn't this her op? Wasn't she the one charged with keeping Fiona Gallagher safe? Wasn't she good enough to get the job done without Damiani's interference?

"It's all right, Miranda. I know who the three men in the black car are now." Fiona had a white-knuckled grip around his neck, but her sobs had quieted to deep, stuttering whimpers. "Tell your men to put their guns away around my daughter, Damiani."

David pointed a finger and the two men complied.

Quinn stepped down to the main floor and stood nose to nose with the big man. "And if you ever speak to Miranda in that tone again, you'll answer to me."

"I can take care of myself," she argued weakly, heartened by his defense of her, yet a little ticked that he thought she couldn't stand up for herself.

"This is my fault," Quinn apologized. "I shouldn't have expected them to simply go away."

Sergeant Delgado's voice buzzed over the radio again. "We're ready to come in."

"Get the door," David told his men.

"What is going on?" she demanded. "We have intruders and nobody's getting you and Fiona out of here?"

"Holster your weapon," Quinn ordered.

Miranda opened her mouth to protest being spoken to with the same superior disdain that he'd addressed

David with. But she snapped her lips shut. Right. Make-out session in the kitchen didn't happen. Tender looks and cuddling in bed meant nothing. She was the hired help. The nanny. She took orders from Quinn Gallagher just like everyone else around here.

Fine. If he wanted a cop, she could be a cop. She secured her gun at the back of her waist. "I'm still waiting for an explanation about the alarm."

"Take Fiona upstairs."

That was his answer? She willingly took Fiona's slight weight when he placed her in Miranda's arms. "Quinn?"

"I didn't think he'd come to the house when I called."

"Who?"

"They're here, sir," Holmes reported.

"Open the door." David pulled the front of his jacket back behind the grip of his Beretta and let his hand rest on the weapon holstered on his belt. "Slowly."

Resigned to the role of protecting the daughter, even though the father was making that difficult to do, Miranda carried Fiona up the stairs. She stopped halfway up when the front door opened at her feet and Rafe Delgado stepped in. He had a hodgepodge of confiscated weapons tucked into his flak vest and utility belt.

Two men in suits and coats walked in behind him with their hands folded on top of their heads. One of them was limping. Holden Kincaid came in, his hand beneath the elbow of a frail gray-haired gentleman.

The older man glanced up as soon as the door was closed and locked behind him, giving her a glimpse of pale gray eyes. Recognition jolted through her. Instinctively, she turned Fiona away from the captured intruders. But Miranda couldn't take her eyes off the haunted paleness of an obviously ill man. "That's him. That's the man I saw in the black BMW out front."

Vasily Gordeeva.

"May I see her?" he asked, his voice thickly accented and sad. "May I see my granddaughter?"

Chapter Twelve

1 Day until Midnight, New Year's Eve

"Why would you threaten her? She's your own flesh and blood."

Quinn had sat up most of the night in his office study, getting to know Vasily Gordeeva, learning a lesson in Lukinburg history and avoiding the occasional accusatory glare from Miranda. She sat on one of the black leather couches with Fiona and Petra wrapped up in a throw blanket and sleeping in her lap. Vasily's two "extended family" members had agreed to retire to the kitchen where they shared coffee, a snack and a lack of scintillating conversation with David Damiani and the two other men assigned to guard them. Rafe Delgado and Holden Kincaid stood in the hallway, waiting to escort Vasily and his associates straight to the airport to put them on a plane back to Lukinburg.

Quinn adjusted the pictures of Val and Fiona and himself on the mantel, then moved each frame back into its original place before turning to his father-in-law. "I can understand you having a vendetta against me, because my wealth made Val a target, and that got her killed. But Fiona—"

"I would never harm my granddaughter. I came to America specifically to see her, to perhaps spend a few hours with her—my last remaining blood relative—before I die of this cancer." Vasily sat at the opposite end of the sofa from Miranda, his fingertips touching the edge of the blanket that covered Fiona. He barely looked strong enough to sit upright, much less strike fear into the heart of the Lukinburg government and its citizens after spending nearly two decades in prison. "I am sad, yes, that Valeska did not live long enough to see me out of prison. And I read the papers. I know about the Rich Girl Killer and that he blamed my daughter—your wife—for his failures. I do not hold you responsible." He stroked the fringe on the blanket without ever once touching or disturbing Fiona. "But I am gravely concerned that you believe I would harm the child."

"Somebody wants to."

Vasily stroked his thinning beard, thinking for a moment. "Nikolai."

"Nikolai Titov? Why? I do business with him. There's nothing personal between us."

"This could be my fault," Vasily admitted. "When I was released from prison, I asked my associates to find out all they could about you and my daughter in the States. Choices I made as a young man took the people I loved from me. I had money, power. But after so many years alone in a cell, I realized I had nothing. In these last days, I wanted to find my family again."

"I'm sorry you're dying, Vasily. But you and your *associates* aren't exactly people I want around my daughter." Quinn sat in the wing chair across from the couch. "But tell me about Nikolai."

"My inquiries may have, as you say, put you on his radar."

"I've made millions of dollars for that man. How can he have a grudge against me that would justify threatening Fiona?"

Vasily shook his head sadly. "There are other things in this world of far more value than money, Quinn. Family. Freedom."

"Nikolai," Quinn prompted. If Vasily had answers, he needed them. "Why would I be on his radar?"

Vasily stroked the blanket again, his gaze lingering over his sleeping granddaughter. When he looked at Quinn again, there was nothing wistful nor ailing in those sharp gray eyes. "You do not know about Nikolai's son?"

"I didn't know he had a son."

"I do not suppose our newspapers are as common reading across the ocean as yours are for us." The old man slowly pushed to his feet. He buttoned his suit coat and straightened his tie before crossing to the mantel to see the pictures of the family he barely knew. "I have heard from a reliable source that Nikolai Titov used your plant in St. Feodor for more than the production of the munitions you created there."

"I suspected as much. The shipping numbers never did add up for a facility that size. That's one reason I closed the plant, though we could never prove anything. What was he funneling through there—drugs?"

"He contracted with arms dealers to move their illegal arms along with your shipments. Very easy to get through customs with your clearance."

Quinn gripped the arms of the chair and channeled his rage into the leather upholstery. Fiona's life was in danger because of some greedy bastard in a foreign country? And he had the nerve to show up in his office? To wine and dine his assistant? "The clock is ticking, Vasily," Quinn urged. "Whatever it is, get to the point. Why would Nikolai Titov want to play this crazy game of 'make it right' with me? What do I have to make right?"

Vasily traced his finger along a photograph of Valeska holding their infant daughter. "The men Nikolai worked with blamed him for the five million dollars they lost when the plant closed. They kidnapped his son and demanded he repay them."

"Five million dollars?" The extortion numbers added up. Quinn rose and joined him at the fireplace. "So Titov takes my five million and gets his son back."

"Not exactly."

A softer voice entered the conversation, the voice of a woman who seemed able to figure out the pieces to a puzzle when Quinn could not. "What happened to Nikolai's son?" Miranda asked.

Vasily nodded at her perception. "Your plant closed more than a year ago, Quinn. Nikolai could not make the restitution they wanted. So, after seven days…they killed his son."

Miranda's gaze shifted to Quinn. The fear he read there matched his own. "There are seven days from Christmas to New Year's. This game, these threats... he's making everything match the same time line he went through with his son. Maybe the bomb, the threats he's sending, are the same things he went through."

"And Ozzie Chang was the inside man he used to get the access to me and GSS he needed."

Miranda scooted out from beneath Fiona's sleeping head and pulled out her cell after carefully tucking the blanket around her again. "We need to get on the phone with KCPD or the FBI. They need to find Titov and arrest him or deport him."

"That son of a bitch." Quinn hurried to his phone to place a call that would wake up Elise Brown. She was the last person he knew to see Titov in Kansas City. He had twenty-four hours to track him down and stop him before he did to Fiona what he'd done to Ozzie Chang and those guards at the Kalahari plant. "I ran a legal business there. He used my company for his illegal activities, but he blames *me* for his son's murder?"

Vasily Gordeeva might be the only person in the room who truly understood that kind of retribution. "An eye for an eye. A child for a child."

THE SNOW WAS BLINDING IN THE afternoon sun as Quinn stood in the concourse at the Kansas City International Airport and watched the plane carrying Vasily and his associates back to Lukinburg take off. The FBI agents who'd processed them and put the three men on the plane were talking on their phones while Quinn watched, until it was just a speck in the clear blue sky.

Taking pity on a dying man, he'd given Vasily the picture of Valeska and Fiona from the mantel. The old man had kissed him on each cheek, and promised that the hours he'd spent with his granddaughter in Kansas City were a true gift that would not be forgotten.

Fine. Quinn could use the good karma, judging by the icy looks he'd gotten from Miranda since the security alarms had cut short that fiery encounter in the kitchen. What a hell of a time for his emotions and libido to take over his rational thinking. As much as they both seemed to be willing to explore whatever was happening between them, it wouldn't have been fair to her to have let it go all the way. Quinn's emotions were a jumble right now, and the fear he felt for Fiona's safety was as potent as the need he felt for Miranda. His anger at Nikolai Titov and his resentment of Vasily for asking questions about Fiona that had given Titov this sick idea of payback in the first place were mixed in there, too. How was that fair to make love to a woman, to think about having a real relationship with someone besides his wife, when Quinn wasn't sure what he was feeling at any given moment?

He needed Miranda to focus on protecting Fiona just as much as he did. Any hurt feelings or misunderstandings or errant hormones sparking between them didn't matter—couldn't matter—until this nightmarish game was over and he knew his daughter was safe.

He'd given a picture and been given a promise in return.

He'd met a unique, fascinating, wonderful woman who just might be crazy enough to feel something for him, too—and he had to let her go. He had to put his daughter first and ignore the ache in his chest and the hurt in her beautiful green eyes.

One threat down. Vasily's spying explained the recurring appearance of the BMWs. His former father-in-law had apologized profusely for drugging the guards in an attempt to get inside the gates, and he had promised Miranda that his men would be severely chastised for shooting at her and running her down with the car. Apparently, he'd had nothing to do with the mysterious package and the bloody doll and the bomb. His search into locating his granddaughter had caught the attention of the man who did, though.

One threat to go.

Quinn's security team was on full alert. Every system had been checked and rechecked. Michael's SWAT team was positioned around the outside walls of the estate. And Miranda was with Fiona.

No one on the planet was safer than his daughter.

He was going to have to disappoint his enemy. Titov could drain Quinn's bank account if he wanted. But no way was he going to *make things right* by tomorrow. Or ever. No way was he sacrificing Fiona to assuage another man's grief and rage for his murdered son.

Now he had to get home and hold his daughter in his arms until the danger outside their home had passed.

Both the FBI agents paused in their conversations on their phones. "Are you sure?" one asked.

"There's no record of him getting on a plane or a boat? Or slipping over one of the borders?"

Feeling a dread as cold as the marble floor beneath his feet, Quinn demanded answers from the two men. "You don't know where Titov is?"

The first one disconnected his call. "If he left the country, he was using an alias. We haven't been able to track him."

The second agent took Quinn by the arm and led him toward their car, parked outside on the circular curb. "We need to get you to a secure location, Mr. Gallagher."

"You need to get me home."

As soon as they were on their way, Quinn called the house.

David Damiani answered. "Sir?"

"You keep eyes on my daughter at all times. Tell Miranda and Michael Cutler and your men. The Feds can't find Nikolai. He could be anywhere."

24 Minutes until Midnight, New Year's Eve

THE FIRST POP SOUNDED LIKE the illegal fireworks the neighbors down the block were setting off to celebrate the coming New Year. Miranda blinked her eyes open to make sure Fiona was still sleeping soundly and checked the time. She wondered if the game would truly end in twenty-four minutes—or, if Nikolai Titov's idea of making things right wasn't met, the New Year was when the real nightmare would begin.

Miranda shifted in the rocking chair, crossed her

booted feet and pulled the afghan up around her neck before dozing off again. Why was she so sleepy? Sure, she'd had some late nights this week, and some emotional ups and downs that had drained her. But she was the last line of defense between Fiona and the horrible thing Titov wanted to do to her. She needed to get on her feet and shake off this terrible fatigue.

Miranda sat bolt upright at the second pop and immediately paid the price for the rapid movement with the pinball machine playing inside her skull. "What the hell?"

She could smell it now—the faint tinge of something sulfuric in the air. She squinted at the yellowish mist swirling beneath the hallway door. Oh, my God. This was some kind of gas attack, an airborne sleeping drug that was slowly stealing her consciousness from her.

"Miranda?"

She heard Quinn's voice calling from the hallway. Then she heard a couple of thumps before something big crashed onto the carpet outside the door.

"Quinn?" She pushed to her feet and stumbled to the bed to hold her hand beneath Fiona's nose. Good. She was still breathing. So far it was just a sleeping gas and not something more deadly.

Her legs felt like putty, her feet like lead weights as she grabbed on to the bedposts and pulled herself around the bed. Quinn was in trouble out there, but they all would be if she passed out, too. She changed direction and headed toward the windows on either side of the bookshelf.

"Miranda?" The door swung open and Quinn collapsed to the floor. He was wearing nothing but his glasses and the sweatpants he slept in. He pushed the door shut and stuffed his robe into the opening at the base of the door. "Gas…coming…from downstairs. Is she…okay?"

"We need air." She fell against the bookshelf, hitting her injured arm. The sting of pain shooting up her arm and down into her fingers revived her for a moment. "We need to get a window open."

"Fiona?" Quinn was crawling across the carpet now, pulling himself toward his daughter.

Miranda unlatched the first window and tried to raise it. But she was so weak. Her knees buckled before she could reach the second window. They were all alone. She was alone. Always alone.

As the blackness threatened to overtake her, she heard a sharp voice. "Miranda!" Quinn's voice. Quinn needed her. "You can do this, sweetheart. Save her."

Fiona needed her.

"Save her."

She wasn't failing the people who needed her again.

Reaching up, Miranda grabbed the edge of the bookshelf. She pulled herself up high enough to grab the window ledge. She got her feet beneath her and pushed with her legs to stand. But the window was so heavy.

In a burst of strength that came from determination alone, Miranda pulled herself up higher, climbing the shelves with her hands, one by one, reaching up to the top of the shelf and feeling around until her fingers closed over the grip of her Glock. *Tick. Tock,* the cruel voice inside her head warned. Time was running out.

Air. They needed air. They were passing out. Maybe dying.

Her hands, trained by the best, trained to be the best, knew what to do even when her eyes refused to focus. Miranda unhooked the holster and dropped it. Her palms folded around the grip, her finger slid against the trigger. She raised the heavy gun and fired three shots at the window, shattering the glass.

Cold night air rushed into the room, clearing her head as she breathed it in. She tucked her gun into the back of her jeans and found the strength to slide over to the other window and open it. The curtains fanned out into the room, telling her the sweet, fresh air from outside was filling the room.

She heard another pop. Her ear jerked to the sound. From somewhere inside the house. With her head clearing, she identified the three pops immediately.

Gunshots.

They were in trouble. Big trouble.

And she'd just announced to whoever was in the house that he wasn't the only one here armed with a weapon.

"Quinn? Quinn!" Growing stronger with every breath, she stumbled back into the room and knelt down beside his still form. She rolled him onto his back and spread her hand over his chest. "Thank God."

There was still a strong heartbeat.

"Quinn?" She tapped his cheeks, tried to rouse him. "Quinn, wake up. We have to get out of here. Someone's in the house."

She rose to her feet and pulled on his arm. But all she

managed to do was turn him sideways. He was too big for her to drag outside. And away from the windows, she was falling under the influence of the knockout gas again.

"I'll come back for you." She stooped down and pressed a kiss to his mouth. "It's my job, right? I'm going to take Fiona outside. I need you to breathe in the fresh air and wake up while I'm gone, okay?"

He moaned something unintelligible.

She leaned in closer. "What's that?"

"Go. Save her."

"I will. I promise I will."

She could hear footsteps all the way down in the basement level. How had Titov or one of his men gotten into the house? There were guards, gates, cops, codes.

"Come on, sweetie." Miranda wrapped Fiona up in the afghan from the rocking chair and carried her sleeping body to the open window. She kicked out the screen onto the second-story porch.

The footsteps were in the hallway now. Anyone who could move that quickly had to be immune to the gas. A standard-issue gas mask would suffice.

"Quinn!" She turned and whispered desperately. "He's coming."

He was on his hands and knees now. "Go."

"He has a gun."

He pushed himself to his feet and leaned against the bedpost. "Systems must be…offline." He lurched to the next bedpost. "No lights. No alarms."

That was right. The house was deathly quiet. There was no movement outside. She'd fired three shots straight out the front window. This place should have been locking down like Fort Knox. Guards from the front gate should have been storming the house. But it seemed every technical gadget Quinn had put into place was dead.

And then she understood what he intended to do. "No. You come with me. When we get outside we can call for backup."

The footstep hit the first stair.

"Come with me," she begged, panic clearing her head now. "We can run to the gate. Climb over it somehow. Forget your security system."

"I can fix it."

She stepped back into the room. "Then I'm staying with you."

He pushed her right back to the window. He bent his head to kiss Fiona. "You save my daughter. That's why you're here." His blue eyes were clear as he captured her face in his hands and kissed her hard on the mouth. "I'm sorry our timing was off. I didn't know I was ready for another relationship until I met you."

Footsteps. "Quinn."

He freed her ponytail from where it was wedged between Fiona and her chest, and smoothed it down her back. "I owe you a proper New Year's kiss," he promised. "But first I'm going to take this bastard down."

He lifted her out onto the porch and disappeared inside Fiona's closet just as a shadowy figure filled the doorway.

MIRANDA RAN THROUGH THE snow, shutting down her emotions, allowing herself no opportunity to think about Quinn trying to be a superhero when he just needed to be Fiona's daddy.

She was across the bridge before Fiona stirred in her arms. "Wandy?"

"Thank God." She kissed her soft forehead. "Randy loves you, sweetie. Be still. Be quiet."

Where were the lights of the front gate?

"I'm cold."

If she thought about it too much, Miranda was, too. But she had to get Fiona to safety. Nothing else mattered.

Except getting back into that house to help Quinn.

She saw a large, dark shadow moving behind the bars of the gate and she instinctively zigzagged off the driveway and plunged into the snow again, making it tough for a potential enemy to get a straight shot at her.

"KCPD!"

The shadow called out at the same time Miranda shouted, "Identify yourself!"

There was a huff of relief and then the beam of a flashlight hit her in the face. "Murdock?" The light instantly lowered. "It's Holden Kincaid and Trip Jones."

She saw the second figure, an even bigger shadow in the darkness, working with a flashlight over by the thick brick wall. "I can't get anything to work," Trip groused. "What the hell is going on? We heard gunshots."

Looping Fiona's arms around her neck, Miranda jumped to her feet again and met the two SWAT cops at the gate. "How many?"

"Three."

She shook her head. "That was me." The house must be soundproofed. "I had to bust out a window. There's some kind of sleeping gas inside."

"The gate's locked up tight." Holden wrapped a black-gloved hand around one of the unyielding bars of the gate. "We can't get in unless we scale the wall or cut through these with a torch. The sarge is coming with the van and some rope."

"Do either of you guys have a spare radio and a gear bag?" There was no way either of the big men could squeeze through the bars, but she had a little three-year-old who could. "Here. Take her."

"Wandy?" she whined.

"You're fine, sweetie. I need you to be a big girl for me." She handed Fiona through to Holden on the other side. "Got her?" Funny, trusting this most precious gift to the man she'd feared was back at KCPD to replace her. Maybe he still was. But tonight, that didn't matter. Tonight, they needed to work together as a team. "I have to go back in and help your daddy."

"Hold up. You don't go anywhere without a sit-rep," Trip chided. He thrust a radio and earbud through the gate. "Alex and the captain are on their way. Captain said all of Damiani's guards missed their check-in. They went to find them."

Intel. Routine. Communication. Training. They were all part of being on SWAT. It was the only way to get the job done quickly and safely, and Miranda intended to do both. She gave a quick situation report while she clipped on her radio and tested it. "Somebody's hacked into the security system here. Everything's offline. Quinn's trying to fix it."

"Here you go." Trip unzipped a gear bag and started passing equipment through the gate. Flak vest. Flashlight. Gloves. Watch cap. Spare clips. Second weapon. Gas mask.

Miranda suited up. "There's someone in the house. He's armed. I heard three shots besides my own. I'm going back in."

"Wait for backup," Trip insisted. "We'll get the gate open."

"There isn't time."

"Murdock," Kincaid warned.

She swung back around and pointed a finger at him. "If anything happens to that little girl, I will come back and kick your ass."

And then she was running, retracing her steps through the snow and across the bridge.

"Can she do that?" She heard Kincaid's voice in her ear.

"Oh, yeah." There wasn't a doubt in the world in Trip's tone.

Now she just had to believe it, too.

MIRANDA CLIMBED BACK UP the railings and decorative posts to reach the second-story porch. Moving as silently as the breeze itself, she sidled up beside the broken window and held her breath, listening for any signs of movement inside. Nothing. Then she stooped down and lightly sniffed the air around the window. She couldn't detect the sleeping gas.

She tapped her radio and whispered, "I'm going in."

"Roger that." Captain Cutler's deep voice startled her. Then reassured her just as quickly. "You'd better be coming out, too. Delgado's here with the climbing gear now. Jones and Taylor will be there to back you up in two minutes."

"Yes, sir." She inhaled a deep breath. Two minutes was an eternity when an officer was storming a building in search of a hostage. This was all on her. Saving the man she'd fallen in love with was all on her now. She couldn't fail. "Going to radio silence. Now."

She turned off the radio and climbed inside.

Fiona's bedroom was empty. Miranda checked the closet and the panic room located inside. That must have been where Quinn had been headed. The door stood open, as if he'd tried to take refuge there. But a quick check showed it to be empty, too.

Miranda fought off the fear that tried to take hold. She needed to think clearly right now, for her own survival as well as his. An empty room meant there was every chance Quinn was still alive, that the man who'd been at the door when she'd escaped with Fiona hadn't killed him. Maybe he hadn't even intended to kill him. Maybe that man had been one of David Damiani's security guards, or Damiani himself, who'd managed to get a gas mask on so that he could find the occupants of the house and get them safely to breathable air.

Yes, think like that. Be positive. Damiani's men were here and—she shined the flashlight on her watch—her own team would be here to back her up in a minute and a half, give or take.

Moving to the door, she checked the hallway for any signs of movement. *Clear,* she sounded off inside her head. She made quick work of the upstairs rooms. *All clear.* Wherever the shadow had taken Quinn, wherever he had gone, it wasn't up here.

She moved quickly down the stairs to the first floor to do a methodical room-by-room search. It didn't take long before she found her first body. She saw the legs sticking out on the far side of the kitchen table. "Quinn?"

Her heart plummeted to her toes as she raced forward. She took a breath of relief. Shirt. No sweats. Not Quinn. She took another breath and frowned in apprehension. This was Rowley, the blond-haired guard, murdered execution-style with a bullet in the middle of his forehead.

She found Holmes at the garage door entrance. Same bullet hole. Same kind of dead. They'd definitely missed their check-in.

But still no Quinn. There was no way out of this house, no way off the grounds with her team closing in.

Miranda checked her watch. Four minutes till midnight. Trip and Alex should be over the wall by now, coming in to back her up. She needed to brief them on what to expect. The sleeping gas had dissipated. There was a dead guard at each exit. No live bodies and one floor left to check.

She tapped her radio, then just as quickly tapped it off when she heard voices coming from the security command center downstairs. She covered her mouth and swallowed her cry of relief. Quinn.

"I knew there had to be a mole in GSS somewhere. Nikolai had the motive, but he didn't have the means to get into my personal systems to send those messages or plant the bomb or take down the security of this house." She tried to pinpoint the source of the sound and finally looked down. She was hearing him through the ventilation duct in the floor. Was there an alternative way to get into the command center without going straight down the stairs and possibly walking into an ambush? "You didn't answer me. And I don't like unanswered questions. I get why Titov wants me dead, why he wants to kill my daughter. I don't like it, but I get it. Why are *you* doing this?"

She heard another voice, infinitely more troubling, as it answered. "Because he's paying me an obscene amount of money. And," David Damiani added, before Quinn could interrupt, "I wanted to prove I was better than you."

QUINN HADN'T MADE IT TO THE panic room as he'd briefly intended. But he'd provided enough of a distraction when he'd tackled David Damiani and knocked that gas mask off his face that Miranda had been able to get Fiona safely out of the house and beyond David's reach before he even realized they were gone.

Now he had a cracked lens in his glasses, a swollen black eye and a few other bruises to remind him just how long it had been since he'd taken down a bully with his bare fists. Despite his broken nose, Damiani had hauled him straight down to the estate's command center, as he'd hoped, and tied him to the chair farthest from the security monitors, but closest to the satellite feed station.

Quinn prayed that David was so caught up in his own ego that he'd forgotten who'd built this room in the first place, and that Miranda was as good a SWAT cop as Michael Cutler—as *he*—believed her to be.

He eyed the clock on the wall. He had a minute left to play this game. "What happens if you don't finish the job by midnight? You're never getting your hands on my daughter. Is Titov going to let you get away with that?"

"What makes you think I still can't get to Fiona?" he taunted. The man's skull was about as thick as that bulletproof vest he wore. "In a few minutes, you'll be dead and I'll be the last, lone survivor of a terrible home invasion that destroyed the great Quinn Gallagher. It'll be in all the papers. People will pity me or think I'm a hero. But I'm going to walk out of here. And you're not. I've planned for every contingency. Even your mouthy loose cannon of a girlfriend will be taken care of." He edged closer with the Beretta in his hand pointed at Quinn's head. "You think I don't know she's coming for you? I'm banking on it. No way can she get to you without coming down those stairs and coming through me first. And I'll be waiting for her."

"Are you sure the five million dollars is for you, David? Where is Nikolai, anyway? Still in the country? At the Swiss bank, counting his cash?"

"Seriously? He's already in St. Feodor, watching this all on TV. A whole ocean away is a pretty good alibi, don't you think?" His denasal laugh as he reached over to turn on the satellite feed was more pitiful than intimidating. "Nikolai, my friend." The blur of Titov's black-and-silver goatee came into focus on the screen. "I have your prize." He pressed the muzzle of his gun against Quinn's forehead. "Shall I do him now?"

"You must wait." Nikolai pulled up the sleeve of his jacket to count off the seconds on his watch. "My son was killed at midnight. It will be the same for Mr. Gallagher."

"Whatever."

Despite the deadly risk of his current position, Quinn had to bite down on the urge to laugh. "I'm glad you were smart enough to figure out that the satellite link is on an individual feed from the rest of my systems."

"Thirty seconds, David," Nikolai announced. "I have been waiting a long time for this moment, Quinn. I have enjoyed watching you suffer. You took my factory, my money, my influence in Lukinburg—so my associates took my son. Know this. Once you are dead, your daughter will be easy prey."

"You go to hell, Titov."

"Now, Nikolai?"

"Twenty seconds."

David began to pace, counting off the seconds with every step. "I always wanted to prove I was better than you, Quinn. I'm the security expert that *you* hired. I take care of GSS, which takes care of all those cops and soldiers and little old ladies in the neighborhood. *I* do that. And yet, people bow down to you. They call *you* the brilliant one. Well, let me tell you something, boss." He got right in Quinn's face. "I can outthink you when it comes to security. Maybe I should start my own security empire. I can afford to now, you know. I planned it all out. I was ahead of you every step of the way. I took your money. I took out your computer codes at GSS and here."

"Ozzie did that—"

"—I got Ozzie to do it. I put a bomb in your building." He waved his gun toward the floors above them. "I took out Holmes and Rowley because, well, I just want their share of the money. It's just you and me, boss. And when the clock strikes midnight, it'll be just me."

"Ten seconds." Nikolai was enjoying this more than he should.

"Congratulations, David." Quinn wanted to keep him talking, wanted the man to confess every little part of their plan since the government monitored all foreign satellite feeds, and somewhere in the country, someone was watching this little show right now. "You came up with a plan to outsmart me, to take out every single device and protocol I've devised. Is that about right?"

"It's eating you up inside, isn't it?"

Quinn shrugged. "You forgot one thing."

"What's that?"

A dusty angel crawled out of the ventilation duct and dropped to the floor behind him. She put her gun to David's skull, and Quinn smiled.

"You forgot to take out the nanny."

Chapter Thirteen

New Year's Day

Miranda wrapped the hotel's fluffy white towel around her and tucked it in above her breasts. She combed out her damp hair and let it fall loosely down her back and shoulders.

"You're a looker," she joked with her reflection in the mirror. "If you're a prize fighter."

She touched the red-and-purple mark on her cheekbone and studied the stitched-up gash in her arm. She started counting all the tinier bumps and abrasions she'd earned while *celebrating* the holidays this week, but lost interest after number twenty.

Now, what exactly was it she had to offer a man again? Besides her heart?

She wasn't sure if it was a case of opposites attracting, or two lonely souls finding each other at a time of crisis, or because he was her comic-book hero come to life, but she'd fallen for Quinn Gallagher in the short span of a week, and had fallen hard.

Work was settling into place for her, she hoped, as

long as she could keep those self-doubts in the past where they belonged. Captain Cutler was writing up a proposal to the commissioner to make KCPD SWAT teams six-man units because it had required *every man and woman on the team to bring everyone safely home.* And she was beginning to think that making Holden Kincaid a surrogate big brother like the rest of the men of SWAT Team 1 might be better than treating him as her enemy. Dr. Kilpatrick was going to have a field day with all the changes going on in Miranda's life the next time she sat down to talk with the police psychologist.

David Damiani had been arrested for multiple counts of murder, including the deaths of his accomplices, Holmes and Rowley. Elise Brown, suffering from an unfounded guilt that Miranda could relate to, had asked for a leave of absence from GSS. Apparently Nikolai Titov's flirtations that she'd found so charming had been a ruse to keep a close eye on Quinn's actions and reactions to each and every threat against GSS and Fiona. And now that there was an FBI and Interpol warrant for Nikolai's arrest, maybe Miranda could take her badge off for a few days to see if she could be the woman Quinn wanted and the friend Fiona needed.

She supposed that new mission started right now.

She opened the bathroom door and walked right into the middle of Quinn's chest. He wore a new pair of sweatpants from the hotel gift shop and nothing else but smooth skin and a dangerous smile. Singed by the contact, her cheeks hot with color, her words stuck in her throat, Miranda retreated a step.

But he followed her right through the doorway, leaning in to capture her mouth in a kiss. "Happy New Year."

Miranda teased him as he pulled away. "You're supposed to do that at midnight."

He shrugged those beautiful shoulders. "I was a little preoccupied at the time." He laced his fingers with hers and pulled her into the main room, where Fiona was stretched out with Petra in one of the room's two queen-size beds. "What do you think?"

Her eyes were on Fiona's sweet face. Oh, to be so young and innocent and to willingly move on from the things that could scare a body right down to her toes. "Is she asleep?"

"She's zonked." He tugged her another step. "I meant this bed."

"Quinn!" she gasped as he pushed her onto the covers and followed her down. His thigh landed between hers, nudging the towel up to an indecent position. Her breast pillowed against his chest as he moved in right beside her. His hands were on her shoulders and face and in her hair. And he was kissing her. And, oh, how this man could kiss. Leisurely. Hungrily. He teased. He took. He lavished. He tenderly invited her to be an equal in every brush of his lips, every foray of his tongue, every gentle nip of his teeth. She was a clinging, grasping puddle of hot, gooey need before she could catch a breath and find her voice again.

"We can't do this here."

"Where do you suggest? My house is closed off as a crime scene. My office has glass walls. This hotel is the perfect place. A locked door. Privacy. Some good friends from SWAT 1 keeping watch outside so we can catch up on our…rest."

"No, I meant…we shouldn't…"

He discovered a sensitive bundle of nerves at the juncture of her neck and shoulder and he teased it with his lips again and again, enjoying how it made her squirm and stammer. He licked the spot and blew warm air across it, raising dozens of goose bumps and making her shiver.

"Damn it, Quinn." She caught his face between her hands and demanded he look into her eyes and listen. "We can't do this here with Fiona sleeping in the next bed."

"You mean, what if you cry out and wake her?"

Miranda caught a taut male nipple between her thumb and forefinger, and grinned as the pectoral muscles bunched beneath her hand and a breath hissed through his teeth. "What if you cry out?" she challenged.

"You are… I can't…" Was the mighty Quinn Gallagher actually at a loss for words?

But he wasn't at a loss for action. As smoothly as they'd fallen onto the bed together, he pulled her to her feet and led her back to the bathroom.

He locked the door behind him and lifted her up onto the granite sink countertop. It was a cold shock to her bottom and thighs at first, but only for a moment. With a sweep of his hands, the towel was gone and his mouth was on her breast, teasing, tormenting. He caught the tip with his tongue and coaxed it to eager attention. His fingers kneaded her hips, her back, her bottom, until they slipped down to her thighs and went suddenly still.

He lifted his mouth from the hard rise and fall of her deep, stuttering chest and looked into her eyes. "I'm finishing what we started in the kitchen last night. Unless you tell me to stop."

Miranda pulled off his spare pair of glasses and gently kissed the puffy bruise beneath his eye. Then she kissed another mark. And another. She kissed his chin. His pulse was beating along his jaw. She laved her tongue around his nipples until he was gripping the edge of the counter and moaning her name.

And then she found his mouth and kissed him there.

She opened her lips to him.

She squeezed a palmful of his butt and pulled herself into his heat, opening her body to him.

He sheathed himself and entered her slowly, filling her, completing her.

He reached over and turned on the shower, but made no move to get either of them wet.

"I don't…" she gasped, clinging to his shoulders, balancing on a precipice of desire and vulnerability, of need and want. "Quinn?"

He grinned. "We'll see which one of us cries out first."

Then, with those blue eyes never leaving hers, he rocked against her and she gasped. She tongued the base of his throat and he spasmed. He flicked his thumb over her nipple and she moaned. She hugged him with her legs and he grabbed up handfuls of her hair as he plunged in deeper and deeper, faster and faster. Their

duel found a rhythm, and a pure molten heat gathered
in the tips of her breasts and weighed heavy at her core.

He kissed her, lifted her, plunged into her slick
warmth, and she cried her pleasure into his mouth as
she crested on wave after wave of aftershocks. And
when she started to tumble over, he stiffened between
her legs and groaned his release against her neck.

And when she was spent and weak and truly sated,
he wrapped her in his arms and she opened her heart
to him.

QUINN SAW MIRANDA GO INTO protector mode one more
time when the bellman knocked at the door to deliver
a mysterious letter attached to a stuffed teddy bear that
was as big as Fiona.

It was difficult to conceal a gun in the pocket of her
red flannel pajamas. And there was no hiding the protective mama posture she had when she inspected the
unmarked gift before letting an eagerly curious Fiona
play with it. Miranda turned her back to the room and
carefully opened the letter as though it might contain
something poisonous or explosive.

When her shoulders sagged after reading the note,
Quinn was instantly at her side. He thought she needed
to sit, but she shook off attention and handed him the
card and a photograph instead. "I'm so glad we didn't
let her see this."

The card itself was brief, but the picture of Nikolai
Titov with a bullet hole in his head and a knife stabbed
into his heart spoke volumes.

Quinn was the one who sank into a chair and needed

Miranda's comforting arm around him as he read the message again.

Quinn—
I am a man whose health is failing and whose history has not always been something a family would be proud of. But I still have some influence in Lukinburg.
I give you this gift.
I will not make further contact with Fiona, as I do not wish for any of my troubles here in St. Feodor to endanger her as they did my daughter. But know that she is safe, and that my enemies, and yours, here in Lukinburg, will never trouble her again.
Someday, tell her that her grandfather loved her. Be well, my son. And be good to the beautiful blonde who looks at you both with such love in her eyes.
Vasily

The three of them had breakfast in bed at about four in the afternoon. It was a messy business involving pancakes and dolls and laughter, flannel pajamas and a newspaper that these two women were never going to let him read.

It was a perfect way to celebrate the New Year, a perfect way to celebrate the terror of the past week finally ending, a perfect way to celebrate the beginning of…what?

Quinn watched the contrast of gold and dark hair

bent together as they plotted some silly plan that probably involved him eating a pancake with his hands clasped behind his back again. He listened to the whispers and laughter. He drank in the smiles.

He couldn't ask Miranda to be his new chief of security. Michael had called her less than half an hour ago with some news that had made her throw her arms around his neck and kiss him. Apparently, no amount of money or charm or personal persuasion on the nearest countertop could lure her away from her job at KCPD.

He couldn't ask her to stay on as Fiona's nanny. He hoped there would never be another call for someone as fearlessly determined as she to step up and protect his child.

And clearly, unless there were some lessons involved somewhere along the line, he couldn't ask her to be the cook.

Fiona needed a mother.

And he needed…Miranda.

If he could just figure out what sort of proposition would appeal to her, then he'd do it. A week wasn't a long time to get to know someone. But he felt more sooner, deeper, differently, with Miranda Murdock than with anyone since his dear Valeska. And it was different than the innocent, rosy-eyed feeling he'd had for his wife. He felt alive, energized, sometimes a little frustrated, but always lucky to be with Miranda.

After Miranda set the tray aside, and Quinn had the chance to sit back and read his paper while they sat together with Petra and read the television listings, he found himself staring.

"What?" Miranda looked up from the grand adventure of a cooking show and tucked that silky fall of hair behind her ear.

"How do you feel about my daughter?" The direct approach might just work with this puzzle of a woman.

Miranda hugged the child at her side. "I've fallen in love with her."

"And her father?"

He'd negotiated million-dollar deals, invented technology on the fly and dealt with people from nations all over the world. But there was no question he'd ever asked where he was this nervous about the answer before.

Miranda smiled. "You're the smart guy, Quinn. Figure it out."

Finally, an answer he understood.

He reached for her hand and they hugged Fiona between them.

"I love you, too."

* * * * *

SUSPENSE

Heartstopping stories of intrigue and mystery—
where true love always triumphs.

Harlequin

INTRIGUE

COMING NEXT MONTH
AVAILABLE JANUARY 10, 2012

#1323 CERTIFIED COWBOY
Bucking Bronc Lodge
Rita Herron

#1324 NATE
The Lawmen of Silver Creek Ranch
Delores Fossen

#1325 COWBOY CONSPIRACY
Sons of Troy Ledger
Joanna Wayne

#1326 GREEN BERET BODYGUARD
Brothers in Arms
Carol Ericson

#1327 SUDDEN INSIGHT
Mindbenders
Rebecca York

#1328 LAST SPY STANDING
Thriller
Dana Marton

*Brittany Grayson survived a horrible ordeal at the hands
of a serial killer known as The Professional...
who's after her now?*

*Harlequin® Romantic Suspense presents a new installment
in Carla Cassidy's reader-favorite miniseries,*
LAWMEN OF BLACK ROCK.

Enjoy a sneak peek of
TOOL BELT DEFENDER.

*Available January 2012
from Harlequin® Romantic Suspense.*

"**B**rittany?" His voice was deep and pleasant and made
her realize she'd been staring at him openmouthed through
the screen door.

"Yes, I'm Brittany and you must be..." Her mind suddenly went blank.

"Alex. Alex Crawford, Chad's friend. You called him
about a deck?"

As she unlocked the screen, she realized she wasn't
quite ready yet to allow a stranger inside, especially a male
stranger.

"Yes, I did. It's nice to meet you, Alex. Let's walk around
back and I'll show you what I have in mind," she said. She
frowned as she realized there was no car in her driveway.
"Did you walk here?" she asked.

His eyes were a warm blue that stood out against his
tanned face and was complemented by his slightly shaggy
dark hair. "I live three doors up." He pointed up the street to
the Walker home that had been on the market for a while.

"How long have you lived there?"

"I moved in about six weeks ago," he replied as they

walked around the side of the house.

That explained why she didn't know the Walkers had moved out and Mr. Hard Body had moved in. Six weeks ago she'd still been living at her brother Benjamin's house trying to heal from the trauma she'd lived through.

As they reached the backyard she motioned toward the broken brick patio just outside the back door. "What I'd like is a wooden deck big enough to hold a barbecue pit and an umbrella table and, of course, lots of people."

He nodded and pulled a tape measure from his tool belt. "An outdoor entertainment area," he said.

"Exactly," she replied and watched as he began to walk the site. The last thing Brittany had wanted to think about over the past eight months of her life was men. But looking at Alex Crawford definitely gave her a slight flutter of pure feminine pleasure.

Will Brittany be able to heal in the arms of Alex, her hotter-than-sin handyman...or will a second psychopath silence her forever? Find out in
TOOL BELT DEFENDER
Available January 2012
from Harlequin® Romantic Suspense
wherever books are sold.